THE
BREAKFAST
CLUB
ADVENTURES

THE GHOUL IN THE SCHOOL

This book belongs to

Books by Marcus Rashford

Fiction

written with Alex Falase-Koya

The Breakfast Club Adventures: The Beast Beyond the Fence
The Breakfast Club Adventures: The Ghoul in the School

And coming soon:
The Breakfast Club Adventures: The Phantom Thief

Non-Fiction

written with Carl Anka

You Are a Champion: How to Be the Best You Can Be
You Can Do It: How to Find Your Voice and
Make a Difference

And coming soon:
Heroes

MACMILLAN CHILDREN'S BOOKS

MARCUS RASHFORD

Written with
Alex Falase-Koya

Illustrated
by Marta Kissi

THE
BREAKFAST
CLUB
ADVENTURES

THE GHOUL IN THE SCHOOL

Published 2023 by Macmillan Children's Books
an imprint of Pan Macmillan
The Smithson, 6 Briset Street, London EC1M 5NR
EU representative: Macmillan Publishers Ireland Ltd, 1st Floor,
The Liffey Trust Centre, 117–126 Sheriff Street Upper
Dublin 1, D01 YC43
Associated companies throughout the world
www.panmacmillan.com

ISBN 978-1-5290-7666-0

1 3 5 7 9 8 6 4 2

A CIP catalogue record for this book is available from the British Library.

Printed and bound by CPI Group (UK) Ltd, Croydon CR0 4YY

To every child who attends Breakfast Club,

this is your starting point.

The world is full of possibilities,

you just have to let your mind take you there.

Welcome to my Book Club.

I'm so excited to share *The Breakfast Club Adventures* with you, a book written by Alex and me especially for you. Take it home tonight and write your name in the front. It belongs to you and only you.

Jam-packed full of adventure, I hope that through this book you can broaden your horizons, you can dream bigger, you can champion and celebrate the difference in one another, and realize that difference isn't a negative, it's a strength.

How boring would life be if we were all the same?

Take the time to ask more questions. Take the time to listen and to learn about one another. When someone is low, our only answer should be to pick them back up. Remember, we all need help along the way.

Enjoy every word at your own pace and remember that there's no rush to get to the end.

Get that head of yours high and let's conquer the day together.

With love,

MR

Chapter One

'Marcus! Marcus!' A voice swam down through the haze of sleep towards Marcus's head, only fully reaching him when it was at its loudest. **'MARCUS!'**

Marcus jolted up in his bed. His mother stood over him, an annoyed look on her face. 'Finally!' she said, throwing up her hands. 'Do you know how late you are for school?'

Marcus looked at his clock and *yelped*.

It was already eight o'clock. He had stayed up late last night working on the case, going over and over his notes, hoping that there was something, *anything*, he'd missed. He'd even fallen asleep with his face pressed against his open notebook, which was now **stained with drool**.

'Sorry, Mum,' Marcus exclaimed as he jumped out of bed and began frantically packing his bag.

'Don't you have that thing at Breakfast Club today, with your investigator friends?' Marcus heard his mum call as he rushed to get dressed.

'**Yes!**' Marcus shouted back. 'That's why I can't be late!' The meeting today was their last chance to solve the mystery. If they got today wrong, it would be *another* failed case.

Marcus gave his mum a kiss on the cheek and ran out of their flat, taking the stairs to the ground floor two at a time. He kept checking his watch as he sprinted out of the estate towards school.

Ten minutes later, he strode into the canteen at Rutherford Secondary School, breathing heavily. He was immediately hit by the sounds of *laughter* from a crowd hovering over a game of Monopoly. For a moment he wanted to walk over and join in, but then he shook his head. He couldn't be late for this meeting.

His two best friends, Oyin and Patrick, gave him a pair of thumbs up as he passed. Marcus grinned back at them. Of course, they knew about today – it was all Marcus had been speaking about for days.

Mr Anderson, the music teacher who was running Breakfast Club that morning, gave Marcus a friendly nod as he walked past, his blue eyes bright and alert. Marcus said, 'Hi, sir!' back.

He made his way over to a table near the back of the canteen, underneath the air conditioner. It was the perfect place for private conversations — just out of the hearing of teachers, and the noise from the air conditioner meant it was hard for other kids to overhear what they were saying.

There were three others there already — Stacey, Lise and Asim, all members of **the Breakfast Club Investigators.** Marcus sat down next to Asim just as Lise pushed a plate of freshly buttered toast and a cup of orange juice across the table his way.

'Thanks, Lise,' Marcus said gratefully. He could see a whole stack of toast over by the kitchen where the canteen workers were getting them prepped. There was still a queue of children, laughing and chatting as they waited for their food. His friends must have gotten here early to make sure he got his slices.

'You're welcome,' Lise said, giving him her wide toothy smile. She tucked her blonde hair, which was partly shaven around the side of her head, behind her ear. Her eyes were sparkling behind her thick glasses.

'Hey, Marcus,' came a murmur came from his left. Asim had a pair of earphones pressed deep within his ears. His dark black hair hung forward over two focused brown eyes as he stared intently at the piece of paper he was carefully sketching on.

'Not a moment too soon! I was beginning to worry you'd miss this – I wanted to run a goblin theory past you before we meet with Gabe.' Marcus raised his eyes from his toast

6

to look at Stacey To, the Breakfast Club Investigators' fearless leader.

'Sorry, I'm late, I oversle—' Marcus stopped mid toast crunch. 'Wait – **goblins?**'

'Gabe's case. It *has* to be goblins,' Stacey said with a confident nod, staring impressively at her fellow investigators. 'They're **mischievous** and they like pulling **pranks**. It's got to be goblins!'

'I thought really hard about it last night but I couldn't come up with anything,' Marcus admitted. 'I think—'

He didn't get the chance to finish. Across the table from him, Stacey's eyes went **wide**. She was looking at something over Marcus's shoulder. Marcus turned to see a short boy walking across the canteen, heading right for their table. Marcus dropped the piece of toast he was holding, and his heart started to beat faster. It was Gabe, the kid who'd given them their most recent case.

'So . . .' Gabe said, sitting down next to Stacey.

'Hey, Gabe, good to see you!' Marcus replied brightly, trying to hide how nervous he felt.

'How's the case coming along?' Gabe said

with a sigh, rubbing his temples.

Marcus nervously glanced over to Stacey. They'd been working on Gabe's case for weeks, but they hadn't had any leads. They didn't want Gabe to know that, though – Marcus was sure they just needed more time.

'Well, we've been looking into it, and we're closer than we were before to discovering why the school bananas are always bruised on Thursdays. We're considering all possibilities –' Stacey paused for dramatic effect – 'even **goblins**.'

Gabe's eyebrows raised at the word 'goblin'. There was a long pause, and then he just said, 'So, you still haven't solved the case.'

Marcus and Lise exchanged an anxious glance.

'We've tried pretty hard,' Marcus said.

'Really?' Gabe huffed.

'It's true,' said Stacey quickly. 'Firstly, we snuck into the back of the canteen so we could see the bananas when they first got delivered—'

She was cut off by Asim. 'No bruises,' he said with a sigh, taking his headphones out of his ears.

'Then we built a small camera with a tracker,' Lise added, 'and put it with the bananas to see if anyone was doing anything to them. It was quite a complicated device – it took me a long time to make it, but—'

'No bruises and no bruis*ers*,' Asim said.

They all looked at Gabe. Marcus was desperately hoping that he would understand how hard they'd tried to solve his case.

Gabe was quiet again, for another few uncomfortable moments. 'But . . . but you're the Breakfast Club Investigators,' he said eventually. 'You solved the mystery of the **Beast Beyond the Fence**.' Gabe gazed at each of them in awe. Then his face dropped. 'I thought this would be easy for you.'

Marcus clenched his fists in frustration.

'Come on, Gabe, you know we can crack this case. We just need more time,' Stacey pleaded.

But Gabe just shook his head. 'It's been over a month! I really need to get to the bottom of this – I mean, bruised bananas are seriously **GROSS**. Sorry, guys – it's probably best that you just forget about the case. Forget I even asked you about it to begin with.'

Gabe got to his feet. 'Thank you for all your help.'

Marcus's stomach dropped. 'A-are you sure?' he said.

'Sorry,' Gabe said again. 'I think this case will have to go to the **Journalism Club**. Maybe they'll be able to figure it out.' And with that he walked away.

Stacey, Marcus, Asim and Lise watched him go.

Marcus groaned.

'It's not a big deal, Marcus,' said Stacey. 'There are always other cases.'

'There won't be any more cases, that's the problem!' said Marcus, annoyed. 'If people think we can't solve cases, then they won't bring us any.' *And without cases the group would drift apart, and then they wouldn't be friends any more*. Marcus didn't say that last bit aloud. He reached out and grabbed the rest of his toast, finishing it in three huge bites. As if on cue, the moment he finished the school bell rang. Breakfast Club was over.

'We need to meet today, after school,' Stacey said thoughtfully. Marcus recognized the determined look on her face.

'At the hideout?' Marcus asked as he got to his feet.

The Investigators began to get their stuff together.

'Yep, it's an emergency meeting. You'll be there, right?' Stacey gave them all a *piercing look*. Marcus raised his eyebrows, but instead of asking what she meant, he simply said, 'Sure' before heading to class.

Throughout the school day, Marcus couldn't

stop thinking about why Stacey had called an emergency meeting. The morning passed with maths and science lessons, and at lunchtime he joined Oyin and Patrick on the football pitch. But even football couldn't help him escape the Breakfast Club Investigators' problems.

Marcus ran onto a cross from Oyin. He was basically one on one with the keeper. Marcus saw his moment and shot hard aiming for the

top corner, but the ball went high above the bar, **missing the goal**. He stood there and watched the ball roll away to the other side of the playground. He bit his lip. He wasn't used to missing.

'Are you thinking about the Breakfast Club Investigators, by any chance?' a voice called. He turned to see Patrick standing behind him.

'Huh?' Marcus replied.

'Come on. You know what he's talking about,' Oyin added as she jogged over. 'You only get that look in your eyes when you're thinking about the BCI.'

'What happened at your meeting this morning?' Patrick asked.

Marcus sighed and put his head in his hands. 'We lost another one of our cases to the Journalism Club,' he mumbled. 'That's like the third one since half-term.'

'That's frustrating, I'm sorry, Marcus.' Oyin put a hand on his shoulder. 'Have you thought about working with them? They seem pretty good at getting to the bottom of things – I mean, they must be doing something right.'

'Work *with* them?' Marcus exclaimed.

'They're **snooty people who** think they're better than us because of that monthly magazine which nobody reads. And, most importantly, they stole our cases!'

'**THE RUTHERFORD GAZETTE**. I read their magazine sometimes,' Patrick said quietly.

Marcus turned to him with a *scowl*.

'I said sometimes!' Patrick added quickly, just as the football came back over. The three of them went back to their positions on the field and Marcus tried to put the Journalism Club out of his mind as they began to play again.

Chapter Two

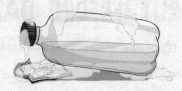

The Breakfast Club Investigators' hideout was a small wooden cabin at the very back of the teachers' car park. The building had been at the school for so long that all the kids had kind of just forgotten that it existed. **It was like part of the wallpaper.**

It had remained empty for years until last term, when their head teacher, Mrs Miller, had warned the BCI that they were getting into too much trouble. Mr Anderson had suggested that the BCI use the shack as a hideout, somewhere they could continue investigating out of sight. It had taken a while for them to fix it up, but they loved it.

Marcus opened the door to find everyone else was already there. Stacey stood in one corner, Asim lay **stretched** out on the couch and Lise was sat on a desk chair, **spinning** around and around.

The hideout had a small table, and on one of its walls Asim had painted 'The Breakfast Club Investigators' in **BOLD** and colourful lettering. On the wall opposite was a map of the school with pins and string stuck to it. Next to that was a giant photo of a bruised banana. Marcus sighed when he saw it. They'd really worked hard on the case.

'OK, let's get started,' Stacey said as Marcus came in.

'This is about Gabe's case, right?' Marcus said. He walked over to sit next to Asim on the couch.

'Yes, but not just that,' Stacey replied, looking serious.

'OK, sure, the conversation went bad, but the case is still open. We can still solve it,' Marcus said, trying to sound more confident than he felt.

'But we don't need to. That's the point.'
Stacey sighed. 'I just wanted to say that if
we're not having fun on this case, then we
just find another one.'

**'But there won't always be
another case,'** Marcus countered. 'We
haven't solved a single mystery since we
found out what was taking the things that
were chucked over the school fence.'

Marcus was, unfortunately, right. That
was the case that had brought the Breakfast
Club Investigators together – their very
first mystery. When Marcus had kicked his
cousin's football over the school fence, it
had disappeared without a trace. Stacey had
invited him to join the BCI so they could
all work together to find out where it had
gone, along with some other things which

had been lost *Beyond the Fence.* At first they had thought that it was a chupacabra, a **giant monster**, taking all the things, but eventually they had discovered that the Beast was a stray dog on the loose, stealing all their stuff. Although Stacey had been disappointed that there wasn't a supernatural creature at the centre of the case, Asim was thrilled – he had adopted the dog after their adventure. Saint was now a fully-fledged member of the Choudhry family.

Marcus sighed. That had been months ago, and since then they'd been given **three whole cases** that they hadn't been able to solve.

'Maybe you're right. It's bad to be a group of mystery solvers who can't actually solve any mysteries,' Stacey muttered.

'Let's talk about it, then. What went wrong with our other cases? The ones we didn't solve,' Marcus said, getting to his feet and holding his hands up. He was starting to feel **VERY HOT**. This all just felt bad, somehow, like they were getting close to breaking up. 'Well, there's the Journalism Club for one. With the **Moving Tree Case** we were *this* close to solving it and then—'

'Journalism Club swooped in.' Asim rolled his eyes.

'They must have it in for us,' Stacey added.

'Really? Do you think so?' Lise said, raising her eyebrow.

'Definitely,' Marcus said, nodding. 'How are they solving these cases anyway?' If he could find a way to stop them stealing their cases, then maybe the BCI would have a chance.

'Maybe we're just **unlucky**,' Asim said, chewing the bottom of a pencil.

'Maybe they have a **SUPERCOMPUTER** that takes in all the information about the mysteries and then spits out an answer,' Stacey said loudly. The room fell quiet. 'It's technically possible,' she added, seeing the looks on their faces.

'Well, maybe we should just ask them . . .' Lise said with a slow shrug.

Stacey and Marcus looked at her disbelievingly.

'Nope,' Marcus said, frowning.

'It might not be a bad idea,' Asim added thoughtfully.

'No way. *They're case stealers.*' Stacey folded her arms over her chest. 'And anyway—'

Suddenly there was a **loud, heavy knock** on the door of the hideout.

Stacey stopped speaking mid-sentence. Everyone **froze**. One by one, they slowly turned around to face the door.

After a few moments, the knock came again.

The Investigators all exchanged quizzical glances. No one ever came to their hideout.

Marcus walked over and slowly opened the door.

A chest. That was all he could see. Someone's chest, and on it was a uniform with a Rutherford school crest. Marcus craned his head upwards. Above him was a smiling face.

'Excuse me. Is this the Breakfast Club Investigators?' the tall boy said.

'Errm, yes?' Marcus replied.

'Good, because I've got a mystery for you.'

Chapter Three

Marcus stepped back into the hideout, and the boy followed him in. He was so **tall** that he had to bend down to walk through the door.

'Is it OK if I . . .' He pointed at a chair.

'Yeah, sure, take a seat.' Lise leapt up from her chair and gestured towards it. The boy walked over, paused for a moment like he was thinking, and then sank into the spinny chair. He sighed with the movement, and so did the chair.

Marcus realized who the boy was – he had seen him around the school gym. It was Gbenga, the captain of the basketball team.

Marcus felt a little nervous – Gbenga was something of a **LEGEND** around school. Marcus had seen him playing basketball before – the whole school had. Last year, the team had dethroned St Andrew's Academy in an amazing win at the Regional Finals. What sort of mystery could Gbenga have for the BCI?

'Hello,' Gbenga said, a little nervously.

'Hi!' Marcus said a little too loudly. He cleared his throat, trying to hide his embarrassment.

'You said you had a mystery for us?' Stacey

said. She was leaning towards Gbenga with a glint in her eye. Marcus had seen this look on her face before – when she had a new mystery in her sights, she was **relentless**.

Gbenga was quiet for a moment, and then he abruptly stood up. 'You know, this is silly. I shouldn't have come,' he mumbled.

'No, you *should* have come,' Stacey said, her voice full of excitement. 'This is exactly the place you should be!'

Gbenga looked at her, unsure. Then he seemed to make a decision. He nodded. 'It's just – it's difficult to know where to start,' he admitted.

'That's OK. Just start at the beginning,' Marcus said gently.

Gbenga slowly sank back down on the spinny chair. He took a deep breath. 'OK, so – Rutherford's Year Eleven basketball team has a **city-wide tournament** coming up. You may have heard. You might have come to some of the practice matches?'

'We've all gone to them, they're really fun!' Marcus said *enthusiastically*. The atmosphere in the crowd when the team was winning was unbelievable. But it wasn't just the crowd that drew Marcus to the games. It was Gbenga – he was *so* good. He moved around the court like a ballet dancer who had the power of a bull. **No one could stop him.** He just made it look so easy.

'Yeah,' Asim piped up. 'Art Club designed the posters for the tournament. They're up all around school.' He looked very proud.

Gbenga nodded. 'If you've been to the practice games . . .' he began hesitantly.

'Well, you'll know we've lost every single one.' He hung his head.

'Yeah,' said Marcus gently. 'I know that

must have been disappointing, but you're still a good team.'

'It's not been the best.' There was a weariness in Gbenga's voice. 'And it's not like us at all – we're used to winning. And, you see – the thing is . . . this is going to sound weird, but the rest of the girls and guys on the team, they seem to think that there's more to the losses than meets the eye.'

'Like what?' Stacey asked eagerly. Her notebook was out, and she was writing in it with a small pencil.

Gbenga hesitated. 'They think we're . . . well, that we're cursed,' he said.

'A cursed basketball team?' Lise said, eyes wide.

'I know it sounds silly. I shouldn't have come.' Gbenga started to get up again, but

Marcus and Stacey reached out towards him. With one hand each on his shoulders, he had no choice but to sit down again.

'No, it makes perfect sense!' said Stacey excitedly. '**Supernatural curses can take many shapes and forms.** We'd be silly to write off the idea that there could be a curse on your team!'

Marcus looked at Gbenga. 'Gbenga, what makes you think the team is cursed?' he asked.

'Yeah, did you open any tombs recently or steal any ancient gold?' Stacey interjected.

'Errm, no.' Gbenga looked *puzzled*. 'The team can tell you more about it. I haven't seen most of it myself, but they say that there have been some . . . **weird things** going on. Things going missing. Basketballs that were here one day and gone the next.'

'Missing basketballs? Is that it?' Stacey stopped writing in her notebook. It looked to Marcus like she was trying very hard not to frown.

'Well, there was also the uniform thing,' Gbenga said, rubbing his mouth. Marcus thought he looked a little embarrassed. He could understand why – **'curses'** sounded silly when you said it aloud. At least it did to everyone except Stacey.

'Some of our uniforms would turn up stained with this **weird liquid**,' Gbenga continued.

'Ectoplasm!' Stacey blurted out. She turned to the other members of the BCI impressively. 'It has to be!' She'd told Marcus and the rest of the Investigators about ectoplasm during their last big case – it was a thick liquid left behind by supernatural beings. Of course, last time, it hadn't *actually* been ectoplasm, just dog slobber mixed with oil, but Gbenga didn't need to know that.

'I mean,' Stacey collected herself before looking back at Gbenga, 'go on, is there anything else?'

Gbenga paused for a longer period of time, like he was really thinking hard about what to say.

'This is a safe space, just tell us what it is,' Marcus said, giving Gbenga a friendly smile.

'Well . . .' Gbenga began reluctantly. 'I haven't seen this, so take it with a pinch of salt . . . but some of the team say that they've been seeing things around the gym.'

'Things like what?' Stacey said.

Gbenga paused, biting his lip. *'A shadowy figure,'* he said finally.

Stacey's
eyebrows
shot up in
excitement.

'Can you describe
it?' Asim asked,
pulling out a
piece of paper.

Gbenga waved
him off sadly.
'I haven't seen it, so I
can't describe it. Maybe
if you talk to the team you
can learn more. Would you
want to do that? I think it
would be really
helpful if we could finally get to the bottom
of this.' Gbenga bowed his head. 'We

really need whatever it is sorted before the tournament starts next Friday – we just can't afford to lose. Is this the type of thing you could investigate?'

Marcus looked around at Stacey, Asim and Lise. His eyes were shining with excitement. 'I think so,' he said.

'*I know so,*' Stacey said loudly.

'There's one thing I don't understand – these mysterious events, things moving and that weird liquid. What did they have to do with you losing yesterday?' Lise asked. 'I was watching the game – it seemed normal to me. Like the other team simply played better on the day – just sport rather than anything supernatural.'

Gbenga scratched his head. 'I think the idea of the curse put everyone on **edge**. We only started losing our matches when these things started happening. It's made the team scared. Made them believe that we're cursed. You've got to stay loose and calm during a match, but we can't do that any more. We've now lost **ten games in a row.** Ten! With this hanging over us there's no way we can win the tournament. It starts at the end of next week. We need this solved right now!' Gbenga said, gripping the end of his knees.

'Don't worry about it,' Marcus said confidently. 'We can definitely help you.'

Gbenga looked up at Marcus from where he was sitting and gave him a small smile. 'I just hope you can manage to solve it in time.' Then he stood up from his chair. 'I'm glad you're on board.'

Chapter Four

Stacey turned to the group as soon as Gbenga was gone. 'I told you. There's always a new case around the corner, and this is a very interesting one. Now, where's that book . . .' she murmured, wandering off to one of the corners of the room.

'Great! A brandnew case.' Lise practically **shivered** with delight.

'I've been waiting for the opportunity to

draw some new things.' Asim grinned as he rubbed his hands together. He reached out to grab a piece of paper from his supply under the table and immediately started to sketch.

'Curses — that's interesting stuff. I think I have a section in here about it.' Stacey was brandishing a book called **An Encyclopaedia of the Supernatural.** The front cover had illustrations of a **werewolf, a vampire** and a **GHOST**. It was her prized possession, which she turned to eagerly during every case.

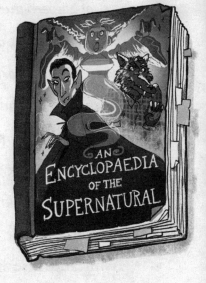

Even though Marcus wasn't convinced about all the supernatural stuff, something about the ritual of Stacey opening the book drew him in. Marcus, Lise and Asim all leaned in, waiting patiently for Stacey to go on.

Stacey flicked through the pages until she found the section she was looking for. '*Curses*,' she read out loud. '*One of the oldest pieces of supernatural lore, which can be seen across the world in a wide range of countries and cultures. At its heart, a curse is quite simple – it is a wish, a powerful wish, for misfortune to affect its target.*' Stacey paused, and looked at the other investigators meaningfully. '*Curses can be powerful. Curses can be* deadly, *and curses affect people's luck.*'

Asim and Lise had **wide eyes** as they stared at Stacey. Despite himself, Marcus felt a cold **shiver** in the tips of his ears.

'What if it's not a curse, though?' he

suggested. 'I mean, last time we thought it was chabachaba and—'

'Chupacabra,' Lise corrected him.

'Yes – a chupacabra – we thought it was a chupacabra and it turns out that it was just a dog,' Marcus finished.

'A very good dog,' Asim added.

'Yes, Asim, a very good dog, but still just a dog,' Marcus said emphatically. 'What I'm trying to say is that there might not be anything supernatural going on at all. There's probably a completely normal explanation.'

'I'm just going with where the evidence is pointing,' interjected Stacey. 'The basketball team say it's a curse, so there's nothing wrong with calling it a curse.' The **twinkle** in her eye was back.

Marcus supposed there was no harm with

agreeing with Stacey for now. 'I guess so,' he said reluctantly. 'So, what do we do next?'

'We have to talk to the team. That way I can get a sketch of whatever creature it is they're seeing,' Asim said immediately. He looked down at his drawing and carefully rubbed something out.

'We should also examine the gym. If they're saying that a mysterious figure is getting in then we should check how, right?' Lise said. She was back on the spinny chair, spinning. 'I'm in Athletics Club, so I know the gym well.'

'Another club? What club aren't you in?' Asim asked.

'Well, I didn't get into Basketball Club. I'm too *short*.' Lise grinned, stretching up her arms to demonstrate.

'We also need to check the uniforms and the ectoplasm on them. That could be a clue too,' Stacey said eagerly. 'It's a great place to start – so let's head to the gym tomorrow lunchtime and check it all out.'

Stacey walked over to the board on their wall. Asim handed her his picture and she carefully took the sketch of the bruised bananas down , then pinned up the new picture in its place. It was a basketball hoop, with a ball soaring towards it. There was a shadowy figure in the background.

'All right, team! Meeting adjourned for today!' Stacey said, clapping her hands.

Marcus couldn't keep a smile off his face on the way home. Maybe a brandnew mystery was exactly what they needed after all.

★

Later that evening, Marcus and his mum were sat in the living room, each with a steaming mug beside them. Marcus had a cup of hot chocolate while his mum had a tea. They each had a book in their hands.

Marcus's mum had felt like they hadn't been getting as much reading done recently, so one day she came home and announced **READING HOUR.** At least twice a week

after dinner they would spend an hour reading together. Marcus quickly found himself **loving it.**

'How's your investigator group going? Any new cases?' Marcus's mum asked as she rested her book in her lap and reached for her tea.

Marcus hesitated. It was like his mum had a **sixth sense** for knowing when something was bothering him. He had been about to open up his own book, but he slowly put it back on his lap. 'Well, we haven't solved that many cases in a while,' Marcus admitted.

'Really?'

'No, but that's all right, because we have a new one!' Marcus grinned.

'Oh yeah?' Marcus's mum said.

'It's to do with Basketball Club,'

Marcus explained. 'Their captain – Gbenga – he came to us himself and asked us to work on the case.'

His mum smiled. 'That's exciting, you were talking about that match recently. He's really good, isn't he, this Gbenga?' She put her tea down again and looked across at him.

'Yeah, he's the **best,** everything just looks so easy for him,' Marcus said, as a Gbenga highlight reel played across his mind's eye.

'I'm sure it's not easy for him – he probably puts in a lot of work.' Marcus's mum raised her eyebrows.

'Maybe a tiny bit,' Marcus shrugged. 'It's been difficult for us I nvestigators recently, but this is where it all turns around, I can feel it. This is a **big case.** We're locked in, finally we have a chance to prove ourselves.'

48

His mum sighed. 'You don't need to prove yourselves to anyone.'

Marcus frowned.

'Marcus?' his mum prompted, after a moment's silence.

Marcus took a deep breath. 'We need cases if we want to keep working together – no one will want to work with us if we just fail all the time. And if we have no cases then . . . our group might fall apart.' Marcus said these last words quickly.

His mum gave him a tight hug around the shoulders. 'Everything is going to be fine. I'm sure your friends aren't going to leave you just because you're not solving mysteries,' she said kindly, before her eyes went back to her book.

Marcus didn't reply.

Chapter Five

At lunchtime the next day, Marcus went to the school gym as planned to meet up with the rest of the Breakfast Club Investigators. His heart was **thumping** with excitement. Their investigation was finally about to **kick off!**

But when he arrived, he saw that the Investigators weren't the only ones there.

In front of them, standing in the doorway,

were a couple of students. Marcus scowled when he saw that they had notebooks and pencils too. He knew immediately who they were.

It was their **nemesis.** The group that had been stealing all their cases.

'Oh look, it's the Journalism Club,' Lise said, arriving at his side with Stacey and Asim. She waved at them.

Marcus's heart **clenched** tight in his chest. It looked like they were going inside the gym.

But just as the Journalism Club were about to enter through the double doors, Gbenga hopped in front of them.

'Sorry, now's not a good time, maybe you can come back later when we're all gone.' Gbenga said. He was standing in front of the gym doors with his arms stretched out. They were so **long** that there was no way past him.

'Why can't you let us in?' a girl asked. 'Is it true that the school basketball team is **cursed**?'

Marcus didn't know any of the members of

the Journalism Club. Despite them competing with the Breakfast Club Investigations, or maybe *because* of the competition, the two groups had never spoken.

'It's a private practice. Please just let us get on with it,' Gbenga practically begged. 'We don't need any distractions.'

The two members of the Journalism Club spun around on their heels and walked back down the corridor, towards Marcus and the rest of the Investigators.

'Oh, hey Lise,' the girl said as she approached. She was short with brown skin and braided hair, and sharp eyes behind a pair of glasses. There was a badge on the chest of her school uniform, which had a pen pressed against a book. The boy behind her was tall, with broad shoulders and a shaved head. He was scribbling furiously in a big notebook.

'Hey Maxine,' Lise replied. 'And Noah.' She nodded up at the boy. He nodded back, before walking quickly after Maxine.

Marcus turned to Lise. 'How do you know them?' He found it hard to keep a tone of accusation out of his voice.

'I used to be part of the Journalism Club,' Lise replied lightly.

'You used to be part of the what?' Marcus and Asim exclaimed.

'What does it matter if Lise was part of the Journalism Club?' Stacey interjected. **'We have a mystery literally right in front of us.** Let's go.' She hurried into the gym.

Marcus shook his head. Lise was the busiest person he knew – of course she had been part of the Journalism Club at one point.

The group followed Stacey through the doors and into the gym. It was a large hall with a wooden floor and a high ceiling, with a line of small windows running around the top of the walls. Big bright lights beamed down from above, shining on the gym equipment scattered throughout the hall.

'Why was the Journalism Club here?' Stacey asked Gbenga immediately.

'They've been **sniffing** around for a while now. Someone seems to have leaked the stuff about the curse to them. Don't worry about it. You're here to talk to the team, right?' Gbenga said.

Marcus looked around the gym. A group of boys and girls wearing Rutherford basketball team uniform slowly **TRUDGED** up and down the basketball court. Even as

Marcus watched, their shots clanked against the rim of the hoops again and again — they were barely getting any in.

'Everyone looks a little . . .' Marcus started. But he couldn't quite find the word.

'Not excited,' Asim blurted out.

'Well, that's what thinking you're cursed will do to you,' Gbenga said. 'It's silly,' he muttered to himself.

'No, it's not. **Curses are serious business.**' Stacey said, getting out her notebook and pencil. Asim and Marcus cast apologetic glances to Gbenga from behind her.

'Anyway, like I said, we have our first game of the tournament at the end of next week. We really need to fix this.' Gbenga looked desperate. 'Is there anything you need to ask me before you look around?'

Stacey tapped her pencil against her notebook. 'To start with, do you happen to know who has access to the gym?'

'Well, the teachers have a key, and all the captains of the other sports teams,' Gbenga said, scratching his chin.

'That's a start,' Stacey said as she scribbled down notes.

'I can write down the names after training, if that helps,' Gbenga suggested.

'Thanks. It would also be great to see the **ectoplasm**,' Stacey said.

Gbenga raised his eyebrows.

'The wet uniforms,' Marcus translated.

'Oh,' Gbenga said, realization dawning on his face. 'Give me just a minute.' He walked over to the changing rooms at the far end of the gym before returning with a bag. Inside, Marcus could see the basketball uniforms, **drenched and heavy with liquid.** He saw Asim make a face.

Stacey leaned in and took a long, hard look at the items. 'Hmmm . . .' she said after a moment. Then she straightened up. 'Yup, this is definitely ectoplasm, of the highest calibre.'

Marcus leaned towards the bag and sniffed.

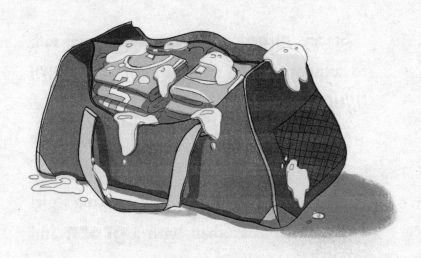

He had a feeling that he knew the smell, he just couldn't remember where from.

'Are you sure?' he asked Stacey. 'It smells familiar, but I can't figure out what it is.'

Marcus glanced around at his fellow Investigators. Stacey had this intense look on her face, like she was desperately trying to figure out what it was. Asim had taken a step back and was now mouthing the word **'gross'**. Lise just frowned at the bag.

Stacey turned to Gbenga. 'Can we talk to someone who's run into **the shadowy figure?**' she asked.

Gbenga nodded. He turned towards the rest of the basketball team and shouted, 'Georgina!' A tall, weedy-looking girl dropped her basketball with a **groan** and came over to where the Investigators stood.

She stood with her arms crossed, her foot tapping against the floor.

'Hi,' Stacey said brightly. 'We're the Breakfast Club Inve—'

'I know who you are. We all do,' Georgina cut in. 'It's good to finally have someone look into this. I just wish it was a group who actually knew how to investigate things, like the Journalism Club.' She shook her head.

'Rude,' Asim muttered.

Marcus sighed. This is exactly what he'd been scared of.

Stacey ignored her. 'Would you currently say that you are cursed?' she asked Georgina.

'Are we cursed? Definitely. **A hundred and ten per cent yes**.' Georgina looked worried. 'You're here to ask about what happened to me on that night. The night I ran into that thing?'

'If you're willing to tell us about it,' Stacey said professionally.

'If it'll help you fix this and get rid of the curse then I'll do anything,' Georgina said.

She took a **deep breath**. 'So – this was a month or so ago. It was late. I'd stayed after school because I wanted to do some extra training. It was around the time that we'd just started having our bad luck in matches, so I wanted to put in the extra practice time and see whether that would help . . . Afterwards I was in the changing rooms, when I heard a **squeaking** sound coming from the gym. So, I stepped out to see what it was. I didn't see anything at first.' Georgina's voice was low but steady. Her words seemed to whisk Marcus away. The squeak of trainers and the thuds of balls hitting the ground all faded into the background.

'The lights were low. I couldn't see the entire gym. That's why I missed it the first time. There was a-a tall, broad **shadow** in the corner.' Marcus heard Lise inhale sharply next to him. 'I could only see it out of the corner of my eye at first, but when I fully turned towards it . . .' Georgina shivered. 'I couldn't see its eyes, but I knew it was staring at me. I just knew.'

Out of the corner of Marcus's eye he could see Asim's shoulders hunch up.

'Then it moved towards me . . . and I just ran. I know it sounds silly, but I just didn't want to take any chances,' Georgina finished.

Marcus swallowed. His mouth felt dry.

'What do you think it was?' Stacey said quietly.

'I don't know what it was, but I know what it means – it means that we're **CURSED**,' Georgina said grimly. 'Ever since I saw that **creature** here things have gone from bad to worse for the team. It *must* have put a curse on us. And I've sometimes even seen the shadowy figure during our games. We haven't won a match in over a month!'

'The thing that cursed the team, that's

what you think you saw,' Lise said in a wobbly voice.

'Maybe it was just a teacher,' Marcus suggested, but he didn't believe it himself.

Georgina shook her head. 'You weren't there. It felt different. It felt . . . I don't know – *evil.* I don't want to ever come across it again. After that, I stopped doing any after-school training, everyone did. No one goes to the gym after school now . . .'

Marcus, Asim, Stacey and Lise exchanged nervous glances.

After a pause, Stacey asked, 'Is there anything else you can tell us? Any ideas you have about what this is?'

'Well . . .' Georgina went on. 'There are rumours. Rumours that something went wrong with Rutherford basketball team in the past. They were cursed by something. I don't know enough about it, but for years people have just referred to it as . . . **the Ghoul.**'

Chapter Six

The next day, the group were sitting underneath the air conditioner at Breakfast Club. Marcus still felt a little bit **shaken** by Georgina's story, and he could see that Lise and Asim were too.

Stacey, however, looked excited. As soon as everyone was there she spread her book of the supernatural in front of the whole group. It was open at a page with the title **'Ghoul'**.

Lise bit her lip, glancing down at the page at an angle, and Asim was tutting at the pictures. But Marcus couldn't look away.

'It comes from an Arabic word,' Stacey said, pointing to the words on the page as she read them. 'It's a creature that haunts graves, hides in the shadows, makes a loud, screeching sound and brings bad luck wherever it goes.'

'*Haunts graves?!*' Asim exclaimed.

'*Brings bad luck wherever it goes?*' Lise shuddered.

'So, this is what we're chasing? Are we sure this is it?' Marcus said, still unsure if he believed it.

'You saw the basketball team yesterday, they sure looked cursed to me. It must be this Ghoul,' Stacey said firmly.

Marcus thought back to the team they had

seen yesterday lunchtime. They definitely didn't look like the team he'd seen win matches at the start of the year.

'It could just be something else, though, right?' Marcus asked weakly.

Stacey ignored him. 'There's only one thing to do now.' She closed the book with a reckless **twinkle** in her eye. Marcus half reached out to her as if he could stop the words from coming out of her mouth, but he couldn't. 'We need to try and see the Ghoul.'

Asim **groaned**. 'Do we? Do we really?'

Stacey ploughed on. 'Last time the Ghoul came out after school, so it follows that the best way to find it would be staying behind after school.'

'The teachers won't like that,' Lise said.

'We just have to not get caught,' Stacey

said loudly, like it was the easiest thing in the world.

'So, we have a Ghoul *and* teachers to worry about?!' Marcus exclaimed. In the shadows of his memory was a warning he couldn't forget: Mrs Miller, their head teacher. She'd threatened to break up the Breakfast Club Investigators before. She'd caught them sneaking out of school, through the fence to the building next door, and had promised them that if she caught them doing anything like that again, she would ban the group. Marcus gulped.

'It's the only way to figure this out,' Stacey pressed.

'I think Stacey's right.' Lise sighed. 'If we want to solve this mystery, then we have to figure out what this Ghoul wants and why it's cursed the basketball team.'

Marcus knew that Stacey and Lise were right. If they wanted to beat the Journalism Club, it was the only way.

'There's just one final thing we need: a way to capture on video or in a photo whatever we find. That way we can know what it is for sure,' Stacey said, *thudding* her fist on the table. She turned to Lise and threw an arm over her shoulders. 'You're our inventor extraordinaire – we need your help!'

Lise nodded. 'It sounds like we're just looking at a motion-activated camera set up. Something that would take a picture of the Ghoul if it appears,' she said.

'I guess so,' Stacey said, sounding unsure. She glanced at Asim and Marcus. They shrugged.

'It shouldn't be too hard. I can probably have it done by tomorrow after school,' Lise said.

'After that's done, **we'll be ready**!' Stacey exclaimed. The other three were silent. 'So tomorrow, we meet in the maths classroom after school, and then we sneak all the way up to the gym.'

'The teachers will be everywhere. That won't be easy,' Asim said nervously.

'We'll make it work,' Marcus said. He was trying to sound more confident than he actually felt.

Stacey nodded in agreement. She took a deep breath. 'So – is everyone OK with the plan?'

There was a *l o n g* **pause.**

Marcus scratched his head. 'No, but I

think if we want to solve this case, then we don't really have a choice . . .' He didn't really think they'd find a Ghoul, but maybe, just maybe, they might find something else that would bring them closer to the truth, to proving themselves, and to keeping the Breakfast Club Investigators together.

Chapter Seven

The rest of Wednesday and Thursday passed in a blur. Marcus felt like he was constantly *holding his breath*. He couldn't believe the BCI were going to stake out the gym after school. He just hoped that they weren't caught by any teachers. *Or* the Ghoul.

By the time the last bell rang on Thursday afternoon, Marcus's heart was in his throat.

Lise had made the motion-activated camera, and now there was just one thing they still needed.

As all of the students milled out of the building around him, Marcus snuck into the nearby toilets. Gbenga was already there, waiting for him.

'Here's the key to the gym,' Gbenga said, fishing in his pocket and then pulling it out. 'No one else should be there today.' He looked at Marcus seriously. 'Be careful. We don't know what's going on here, and *curses aren't to be messed with*.'

Just as he said it, the lights above them **flickered** slightly.

Gbenga looked up at them, then shook his head before dropping the key into the palm of Marcus's hand.

It felt **cold.** Marcus pocketed it. Then he said, 'I just hope we find something. You know, it still feels a bit weird that we're actually working on a case for you. I mean, you're *Gbenga*, the captain of Rutherford's basketball team. I can't believe you need *our* help.' Marcus tried his best to keep the awe out of his voice as he awkwardly **shuffled** from foot to foot.

'I'm glad to be working with you,' Gbenga said, smiling. 'Your team of Investigators is pretty good. I mean, you solved that mystery about the things disappearing over the fence.'

'That was ages ago.' Marcus waved his words away.

'It's still something. Look at us – we've been losing all month. That doesn't make us suddenly bad at basketball,' Gbenga said, although he looked unsure.

Marcus went quiet. He was thinking about what they were about to do. 'But there's still pressure. To do well, I mean. Isn't there?' he asked.

Gbenga gave him a sad smile. 'Yeah, there is.' He started towards the door. 'See you later, Marcus – and good luck tonight. I really hope you find something.' And with that he walked away, leaving Marcus standing in the empty toilets.

Slowly, he made his way to the maths classroom where he had agreed to meet the others, thinking all the while about what Gbenga had said.

Marcus was the first to enter the classroom, followed closely by Stacey and Lise.

'Where's Asim?' Marcus asked the other two.

'He said he'd meet us outside the gym,'
Lise replied.

Marcus frowned. That was weird. He
wondered what Asim was up to.

Marcus, Stacey and Lise huddled together
on the floor so that the crowds of school kids
and teachers in the corridors wouldn't see them
if they happened to look into the classroom.
Very slowly, the crowds dispersed, until finally
there was silence outside.

'Do you think they're—' Marcus started,
but Lise and Stacey immediately turned and
SHUSHED him.

They waited there in silence for a couple
more minutes, and then slowly got up and
cracked the classroom door open. All three
of them poked their heads into the hallway.
After a quick look left and right, it was clear

that everyone had left school.

'Are you ready to find a Ghoul?' Stacey asked.

'I didn't build my invention for nothing. No backing out now,' Lise replied, grinning.

Marcus took a deep breath. 'We're the Breakfast Club Investigators, and this is what we do!'

The corridors were completely empty now. Marcus couldn't remember many times he had been in the school when it was this silent, without the steady rumble of kids talking, footsteps in the corridors or bells ringing. He was left with the sound of the building itself: the deep groans of pipes in the walls as they **expanded** and **shrank,** the rustle of abandoned pieces of paper catching the breeze from the air conditioning. And all the while the sky was slowly turning orange – **IT WAS STARTING TO GET DARK.**

Slowly, they moved through the corridors. Marcus's forehead began to prickle with sweat – he was so nervous that they were going to get caught. He took shallow breaths, trying to make as little noise as possible as he crept behind Stacey. **Every small sound rattled him.**

It took a while, much longer than it would have taken normally, but soon they were outside the double doors to the gym. Asim was waiting for them there, and next to him stood his very large dog, Saint.

'Asim!' Stacey exclaimed. Her shout echoed around the empty corridor. 'Why have you brought *Saint* to *school*?'

'Well, I just thought she'd be useful, you

know, in case we actually do run into the Ghoul,' Asim said defensively.

'**Ugh,**' said Stacey. 'As if we aren't in enough trouble already if we get caught . . .'

Marcus had to stop himself from laughing as he bent down to scratch Saint's ears. Saint **woofed** happily in response.

'My parents asked me to walk her after school, so I thought I may as well bring her.' Asim shrugged. 'She could be good protection!'

'She's here now, so she'll have to come,' said Lise with a smile.

'**Fine!**' huffed Stacey.

Marcus didn't want to admit it, but he did feel a little bit better with Saint around.

He fished in his pocket for the key and put it in the lock. With a small *thunk* the lock released and the doors swung open. For a moment, the Breakfast Club Investigators simply stood there, staring into the dark gym. It looked much more **ominous** in the light of the setting sun, and Marcus shivered as he remembered Georgina's story.

Stacey steeled herself and then marched inside confidently. Asim, Lise and Marcus exchanged gloomy glances and then followed her in, Saint **scampering** behind Asim. They followed the glow of Stacey's flashlight as they crept across the shadows of the gym, trying to be as quiet as possible.

After some furious whispering about where the best vantage point would be, they settled in one of the corners of the gym. Marcus and Lise were crouched behind some **funky-smelling mats,** while

Stacey, Asim and Saint were to their right, hiding behind a bag stuffed full of different types of balls. Well, they were trying to hide. Saint kept dipping her nose into the bag, and pulling out balls to play with. Asim was trying to wrestle the balls out of her mouth, but that seemed to only make her more excited.

Each group had a camera with them, which would capture the Ghoul if it turned up.

From the gym's windows, Marcus could see the sun pulling away from the building, taking its light with it, leaving shadows that darkened with every passing moment. He felt a trickle of **sweat** ease down his back, making him sit up straight.

When would the Ghoul appear?

Suddenly, there was a whisper to his left.

'Are you sure about this plan?' Lise asked. Marcus **jumped** at the sound of her voice.

The silence had been so overwhelming that he had almost forgotten that the others were there.

Once his heart had stopped thudding, Marcus whispered back, 'It seems all right. I guess it'll work.'

'But what if it doesn't?' Lise said. 'Maybe we need to have a backup.'

'Like what?' he asked.

Lise glanced sideways at him. 'Well, we could always ask the Journalism Club for help,' she suggested.

Marcus **blinked** hard. 'Are you being serious?' he said, more loudly than he'd intended.

From their left came the sound of Stacey *shushing* them furiously as Saint thumped her tail against the floor. Saint didn't really get the whole hiding thing.

Lise continued even more quietly. 'Of course I'm serious, Marcus.'

'They stole our cases,' Marcus replied in a furious whisper.

Lise held up her hands. 'They're nice people,' she said. 'If it's going to be *so* bad for the BCI if we can't solve this case, then why don't we just ask for help?' She said it like it was the easiest thing in the world.

'It won't help, and even if it did—' Marcus stopped suddenly at a small scuffing sound. His eyes darted around the gym, following what he thought was a shadow. He squinted – finally he could see it!

It was Saint's tail, wagging. Marcus let out a breath.

'And even if it did . . .?' Lise prompted him.

'Nothing, forget about it. OK?' Marcus said. He wrapped his arms around his body. **He felt cold.**

Lise had this look on her face like she wanted to keep pushing and ask another question. But she didn't.

'Fine,' she said eventually.

A full hour passed in silence, and the Investigators were starting to get restless. Saint's **snores** filled the gym. It was now almost completely dark in the gym, and Marcus could barely see his own hand in front of his face.

Asim, Stacey and Saint walked over to where Marcus and Lise were crouched.

'Maybe we're not going to see a Ghoul today,' Asim said, plonking himself down. Saint licked at his face. He sounded more relieved than disappointed.

'Yeah, maybe we're not,' Lise replied, grimacing.

But nothing could put Stacey off. 'We'll come back tomorrow. I know we'll find it,' she said with a confident nod.

'Yeah, definitely,' Marcus said, despite the nerves in his stomach. He didn't want to admit it to the others, but he was feeling worried that they hadn't found anything yet. What if they were unable to progress with the case?

The group got up from the floor slowly and gathered their flashlights. Lise packed away her cameras. They walked out of the gym and Marcus locked the door behind them. It was even darker in the corridor, after the big windows in the gym that had let in the last of the light.

They had just started to walk down the hallway when Marcus heard it.

Footsteps. **Slow, shuffling, eerie footsteps** were coming from the hallway ahead.

Marcus froze. He could feel his heart *thudding* in his chest. Next to him, he heard Asim **gulp** loudly.

In the gloom, the corridors had changed. The shadows hid the corners of the hallways, making the space look much bigger than it had during the day. It felt like whatever was walking towards them could be coming from any direction.

Saint began to whimper.

Suddenly, out of the darkness ahead of them, Marcus could make out a shape. It was somehow both *tall* and **HUNCHED** at the same time. Human, but not human. Like darkness had been moulded into a form; into something that could walk, haunt, hunt.

It was the Ghoul.

Marcus's body tightened. He knew that he had to move, but it was as if he had forgotten how. It was like there was a wall between his brain and his body, and the signals between them just couldn't get through.

A **terrible, low, warbly moan** echoed down the halls. Marcus felt like it was reverberating all around him, clawing at his very being.

Saint let out a loud, high-pitched whine. Asim spun on his heel and ran, bumping into Marcus as he went, shaking him free of whatever spell he was under. Marcus gasped and quickly spun around too, tearing through the hall with Lise and Stacey hot on his heels.

Saint galloped ahead of them all.

The five of them **thundered** down the hallway, away from the gym. Another terrible *screech* followed them. They raced past classrooms and ran down the stairs two at a time. Marcus's heart was **pounding** in his chest and there was sweat **dripping** from his face. He couldn't stop – he just knew he had to get as far away from that *thing* as possible.

They ran until they were almost at the doors that led out of the school. Marcus stopped, his hands on his knees, gasping for breath, as he waited for the others to catch up with him.

'It's real!' Stacey panted, as soon as she had gotten her breath back. There was a look of complete shock on her face. **'The Ghoul is real!'**

'I think – we just about – got away from it,' Marcus said in between gasps for air.

Suddenly, there was another sound, almost as terrifying as the one the Ghoul had made.

'Got away from what?' called a voice from the corridor ahead. *'Who's there?'*

Marcus's heart dropped. He knew that voice. It was Mrs Miller, the head teacher of Rutherford! He could see her shadow approaching and hear her footsteps echoing through the now-silent hall. 'Who's there?' she called again.

Blood was rushing in his ears. 'This way,' he mouthed to the others. They all looked terrified.

Marcus slowly crept over to a nearby classroom, cracked open the door and then

squeezed himself through. Then he beckoned for the rest of the group to do the same. A moment later Stacey and Lise were crouched behind the door next to Marcus.

Asim was pulling Saint along as quickly as he could. He slipped into the classroom, trying not to touch the door, and tugged the dog in after him.

They kept their mouths tightly shut; Marcus barely dared to breathe as they heard Mrs Miller walk slowly past the door. Even Saint was completely silent.

Marcus let out a long breath as soon as her footsteps faded.

'That was too close,' Stacey whispered.

Chapter Eight

It was hard for Marcus to get to sleep that night. At first the adrenaline felt like **lightning** in his veins. But after a while, when that faded, Marcus began to realize what he was really feeling.

Fear.

He kept thinking back to that hallway. Back to the thing he saw there. He wondered if it had been just his brain playing tricks on him. Had it just been a trick of the light? After all, it had been dark. Maybe the ghoul had actually just been a teacher? Or a student? But that sound it had made . . . what sort of person makes that sound?

Ghouls don't exist.

That's what Marcus wanted to believe. But how could he think that after what he had seen?

Marcus eventually drifted off into a fitful sleep, dreaming Ghoul-filled dreams. He woke up with his sheets drenched in sweat, feeling exhausted.

He entered Breakfast Club still feeling **DAZED.** He was sure that Patrick and Oyin were there, and in the back of his mind he knew that there were kids playing games, having fun, and eating delicious breakfasts, but he couldn't see, hear or smell any of it. Marcus was stuck between his memories of last night and the things he wanted to say to the Breakfast Club Investigators.

'So, what do we think that was?' Marcus said the moment he sat down at the table under the air conditioner.

'Ghoul,' Stacey said, without even a hint of hesitation. She had a steely look in her eye.

'It felt very ghoulish to me,' Lise agreed. She looked very **pale.**

'Was it really? It couldn't have been, because if it was . . .' Asim trailed off. He had **dark circles** under his eyes. Marcus knew that none of his friends had gotten a good night's sleep either.

'But what if it wasn't?' Marcus countered. 'It could have been a teacher?'

'Marcus, you know that wasn't a teacher,' Stacey shot back. 'I know what I saw. And I know that you saw it too. You can't deny it.'

'And we were this close to being caught by Mrs Miller,' Asim said, raising his finger and thumb to demonstrate exactly how close they had come. **He shivered.**

'But we didn't get caught, right, Lise?' Stacey nudged Lise. Marcus couldn't help but think that sometimes Stacey had more fun when things were a little dangerous. 'The real danger was that Ghoul.'

'Either way, we did see something, and it was probably what Georgina also saw,' Lise said, sighing. 'You saw the basketball team practising – if they play like that at the tournament next week they'll get **OBLITERATED.** We have to help.'

'So, we're going to try and find that thing again?' Asim said. He looked terrified.

'We have to,' Marcus said. 'If we can't solve this, then this case and everything else we have will go to the Journalism Club!'

'We'll come up with something.' Stacey nodded. She looked at Lise. 'Did you pick up any camera footage of the Ghoul?'

'No,' said Lise sadly. 'I set up our cameras in the gym. We ran into the Ghoul outside the gym.'

'The Ghoul really is the key to everything,' Stacey said thoughtfully. 'If we could just figure out why it's here, then we can solve this case.' She reached into her bag. 'And this is how we do it.' She **slammed** a piece of paper onto the table.

Marcus, Lise and Asim huddled close and

looked down at it. Marcus had seen this before, hung up around the school.

'Basketball match, this Monday at lunchtime in the gym.' Lise read out the words that were written on the flyer. 'You think the Ghoul will show up here?'

BASKETBALL MATCH

Next Monday at lunchtime in the Gym

Stacey nodded with a sharp-looking grin. 'Remember what Georgina said. She even saw the shadowy figure at some of their games,' she reminded them.

'Why at the match, though? Why not just try and find it at night again?' Marcus said, but the shiver down his spine as he spoke answered the question for him.

'At night we have the disadvantage. We can't see anything—' Stacey started.

'And we'll probably get very scared,' Asim added, looking up from a sketch he was doing.

'Yep, we'll probably get very scared,' Stacey agreed impatiently. 'But also, more importantly, supernatural beings are at their most **powerful** during the night. During the day it's the opposite. If we're hunting it during the daytime, then the Ghoul will be on the back foot.'

Without even thinking, Marcus stood up excitedly. *We might actually have a chance!* he said.

'The only question is, how do we catch a Ghoul?' Lise asked.

'I drew a picture of it. Maybe that will help,' Asim said. He pushed a piece of paper onto the table, next to the basketball poster poster. It was a pencil sketch, with heavy shading that was **moulded into a dark, ominous shape.**

It was a good drawing. It reminded Marcus of what he had seen the night before, and for a moment he was back there in that dark corridor with those footsteps coming closer and **closer and closer . . .**

Asim's voice pulled him out of his memories and back to Breakfast Club. 'There wasn't that much to draw.'

'No, it's helpful! We need to get used to looking at it,' Stacey replied, prodding at the sketch. 'We can't be too **scared** if we're going to catch it.'

'Let's think back to last night. Maybe there's a clue there that can help us,' Lise suggested.

Marcus shivered. If he had to think of those footsteps again, then—

He stopped mid-thought. 'Footsteps!' he

blurted out. 'The Ghoul had footsteps!' The idea flew out of his mouth before he'd even realized what it meant.

Asim frowned. 'But what does that mean?'

'That means it must have weight, it must be physical!' Stacey said with a **TRIUMPHANT CLICK** of her fingers. She pulled out her book of the supernatural and cracked it open. Her eyes scanned the pages, moving so quickly that Marcus was surprised that she could even read the words.

'It makes sense,' she said slowly. 'Sometimes creatures like ghosts can move through the air, invisible, but other times they can take physical form. Then they become able to physically touch things, move things and –' She paused dramatically – 'even **make footsteps.**'

'So . . . does that mean we can trap it?' Marcus asked.

'But what if it turns **INVISIBLE** again and manages to get away from us?' Lise asked.

'We only need to trap it for a moment and – *I don't know* – take a picture of it, or just see it properly in the light!' Stacey exclaimed. 'That might tell us something about the Ghoul and why it's haunting the basketball team.' She began to flick through the pages of her book again. 'Or we can force it to stay there and answer questions.'

'What will we actually need to trap a Ghoul?' Marcus asked.

'We can try what we tried with the chupacabra,' Lise said. Stacey nodded in approval. They had tried capturing the chupacabra in the woods with a sheet and some rope.

'Don't worry, I'll figure it out.' Stacey stood up proudly, before turning and sheepishly looking at Lise. 'And by that I mean I'll take Lise with me and ask her really nicely to help me with the calculations of where to put everything. You guys just need to get the materials.'

'That shouldn't be too hard,' said Asim.

'And stay out of the way of Mrs Miller,' Lise added.

'That'll be a little harder,' Marcus said.

'All right, so that's our plan. The next stop on this ride is the basketball game on Monday,' Stacey said happily.

Marcus, Asim and Lise shared a nervous glance, but eventually they nodded their agreement.

Chapter Nine

Over the weekend, Asim and Marcus decided to meet up to get supplies for Monday. Asim brought Saint along for the walk. She bounded ahead of them, happily sniffing at trees and wagging her tail as she went.

The boys talked **animatedly** about the case, but after a few minutes, Asim turned to Marcus with an unusually serious look in his eye. 'You know,' he began hesitantly, 'I've been thinking. Working with the Journalism Club might not be so bad.'

Marcus turned and gave him a look. **'Not you too!'** he moaned.

'Come on, Marcus, they're not all bad – they even put one of my paintings in the *Gazette* once. They're nice people, mostly. And we might need help to solve this case.' When Marcus didn't say anything, Asim

went on. 'Come on! I'd never had my art featured before. It was cool.'

Marcus kept his mouth firmly shut.

'Let's just talk about it,' Asim pressed.

'Let's just talk about something else,' Marcus grumbled.

'Marcus, I—'

'We don't need help,' Marcus interrupted. He sighed, staring down at his shoes as he walked. 'We just have to stop making mistakes. We have to solve our cases.'

'Making mistakes isn't always a bad thing; sometimes it's a chance to learn,' Asim said slowly and thoughtfully. 'I spend a lot of time painting. I think I'm pretty good at it, but I mess things up every now and again. Even my mum messes up on her paintings every once in a while.' Asim's mum was a **famous** painter who travelled the world working and selling her art. 'But whenever I make a mistake, I think about how I can do better next time, and sometimes ask my mum for help.' Asim smiled. Saint barked loudly next to him, and Asim leaned down to scratch her ears.

Marcus didn't say anything. He knew that Asim had a point, but he was still worried about what would happen to the group if they couldn't solve this case.

Eventually, Asim came to a stop outside of a craft shop called **'The Colourful Canvas'**.

'Why are we here?' Marcus said grouchily. 'I thought we were getting supplies to catch the Ghoul with.'

'Sometimes I help out here on the weekends, and in return Ms Lamont gives me some of the leftover stock,' Asim replied, as he pushed open the door of the shop. Marcus glanced inside. There were paints, brushes and canvases everywhere, all stacked and arranged neatly across a series of white shelves.

The woman at the counter smiled as she saw Asim, and laughed as Saint **BOUNDED** over to her and put her front paws on the counter. She reached down and scratched the husky's throat.

'Hi Asim, hi Saint, how are you?' Ms Lamont asked. She pointed at a basket on the floor, filled with paint bottles, a paint-splattered sheet and a long rope. 'Here are the leftovers from last week and the extra bits for your special art project. I'd love to take a look at it when you're done.'

'Thanks, Mrs Lamont! Errm, yeah, I'll definitely show you when I'm done,' Asim said with a nervous smile. He caught Marcus's eye and grinned. They couldn't tell her that the supplies were really being used to **catch a Ghoul.**

'And how are you doing?' Mrs Lamont turned to Marcus. 'It's so nice to see Asim bringing his friends around.' She gave Marcus a **mischievous** smile.

'I'm doing good,' Marcus replied. 'It's nice to meet you. I'm Marcus.'

He thought about what Mrs Lamont had said as Asim walked around the shop with Saint at his heels.

Friend.

A couple of months ago the thought would have made Marcus laugh. He and

Asim hadn't really known each other before the Breakfast Club Investigators. But now, Marcus couldn't imagine not being friends with him.

And it wasn't just Asim. Marcus really was friends with them all, Stacey and Lise too. And that's why *he couldn't let the Breakfast Club Investigators fail*. He couldn't let the thing that bound them together fall apart.

Chapter Ten

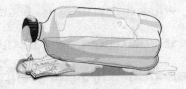

When Marcus arrived at Breakfast Club on Monday morning, he didn't feel nervous. **Determination** coursed through his body as he thought about how they were going to catch the Ghoul once and for all. They needed to get to the bottom of the curse and prove that they could solve cases.

'Marcus, did you hear what I just said?' Oyin's voice broke through his **haze** of thoughts. He looked down to see there was a bowl of porridge in front of him. It was **cold.**

How much of Breakfast Club had he spent thinking?

'Sorry, what did you say?' Marcus asked.

'I asked if you were going to the basketball game at lunchtime. **It's the team's last game before the big tournament starts on Friday,**' Oyin said.

'Yeah, the rest of the football team is going, to show some support.' Marcus almost jumped as Patrick's voice came from his left – he had been so lost in his thoughts he had pretty much forgotten that Patrick was even there.

'I'll be there. Well, maybe for a little bit of it . . .' Marcus trailed off.

'Is this Breakfast Club Investigators

related?' Patrick asked, raising an eyebrow over his thick glasses.

Marcus hesitated. He knew that Patrick and Oyin sometimes got concerned about how far the Breakfast Club Investigators would go. 'Maybe,' he admitted.

'Please don't do anything silly. You know Mrs Miller's going to be there,' Oyin warned.

'Are the Breakfast Club Investigators going to be making an appearance at the basketball match today?' A new voice joined the conversation from behind them. Marcus turned to see Mr Anderson smiling down at him.

'No, Mr Anderson. I mean – yes – we'll be watching the game, but that's it,' Marcus said as he glanced back over his shoulder.

'Good. Mrs Miller is going to be at the

game at lunchtime, as are most of the teachers. If something were to go wrong, then the group that caused that would probably get into a **lot of trouble**,' Mr Anderson said, looking unusually serious.

Marcus frowned. Everyone seemed to know that the Investigators were on their last chance with Mrs Miller.

'Rumours have reached the staffroom that you are investigating Basketball Club?'

Marcus sighed heavily. 'Yes, we're investigating Basketball Club, but no, we're not going to be getting up to anything that could possibly get us into any trouble.' He crossed his fingers underneath the table.

Mr Anderson smiled at him. 'Good. I'd hate to see the Investigators broken up, when I know how much fun you all have together.'

Marcus pushed down the nervous feeling that was **CREEPING** through his stomach.

Oyin, Patrick and Mr Anderson didn't understand. The Breakfast Club Investigators had to catch the Ghoul *so* the club could stay together. And getting caught was just a risk they'd have to take.

★

A couple of hours later, Marcus was in the hallway outside the gym, tying a large sheet to the wall. He **swallowed** hard. He couldn't shake the feeling that something bad was going to happen. But they couldn't stop now.

He looked back at Lise, who gave him a thumbs up.

'Looks good to me,' she said.

It had been easy for them. They didn't go into the school gym with the rest of the kids, and everyone else was so preoccupied with the game that no one had noticed them slip away.

Now the four of them stood in the corridor, setting up as low **groans** echoed out from the gym. It sounded like the basketball team were still having trouble.

'Are you sure this will work?' Marcus asked as he finished tying up the rope.

'Of course this will work!' Stacey replied, walking into Marcus's view. Asim was down at the other end of the corridor, keeping watch for teachers.

'Now we just have to wait around for the Ghoul to appear, I guess,' Marcus said, as he walked away from the wall to survey his handiwork.

'How's the game going?' Lise asked.

Marcus glanced through the crack in the gym door, just in time to see Gbenga take a shot. It **clanged** against the backboard, then the side of the hoop, and then spun away.

There was another loud groan from the crowd. The other members of Rutherford's basketball team sighed, their heads *dropping* as they ran back down the court as the visiting team prepared to attack.

Sporadic claps came from courtside, where both students and teachers looked on

helplessly. The scoreboard read '3-23'.

'It definitely looks like the team is still cursed,' Marcus muttered. Then he heard a sound behind them and turned sharply.

Someone was there.

Marcus's heart started to beat more quickly. *Was it the Ghoul?*

Two people came round the corner, and Marcus exhaled.

'Hello, Lise,' Maxine said as she drew closer. Noah stood behind her, taking notes. As usual, he didn't say anything.

'Hello, Maxine,' Lise replied, smiling widely.

'You're here again,' Maxine observed.

'Almost everyone's here. It's the basketball team's last practice match,' Marcus replied smoothly.

'But you're here all together. The Breakfast Club Investigators. So, you must be . . . **investigating?**' Maxine raised an eyebrow. It was a question, but Marcus could already feel the sureness wafting off her.

He didn't even try to lie. 'We're investigating,' he admitted.

Noah stopped taking notes and stared directly at Marcus.

'I thought so. We're looking into it too,' Maxine said. 'You know, we should share notes. Maybe we might each learn something.'

'Maybe—' Stacey began.

But Marcus interrupted her. 'We don't

need to. Like you said, we're the Breakfast Club Investigators. We'll figure this out.' He **scowled.** 'We don't need any help from case stealers like you.'

'*Case stealers?*' Maxine said, looking surprised. 'You're the ones getting in the way of *our* investigations with – whatever this is!' She gestured at Asim, who was standing in front of the sheet they had hung up, trying and failing to shield it with his body. 'Is that to catch the *Ghoul*?'

'**You know about the Ghoul?**' Stacey yelped.

'You're not the only one who's spoken to Georgina. I know it's a thing that some members of the basketball team believe in. And it looks like you do too,' Maxine said.

'*You're* the ones who get in the way of our

investigations, actually,' Asim blurted out.

'We're going to solve this case and **beat** you,' Stacey said, pointing angrily at them.

'Sure, I bet you will.' Maxine paused. 'But there's a reason we've been solving cases and you haven't.'

Marcus scowled at her again, but none of them asked her what she was talking about.

'Good luck with your plan here,' Maxine said after a moment. Then she walked off, followed by Noah.

'What was she talking about?' Marcus asked after she had left. **'Why does she think we haven't been solving cases but they have?'** No one responded. 'Doesn't anyone know?'

Again, no one replied.

The group waited around in the hallway as time ticked away. Marcus was on edge, all of his senses tuned into the corridor around them. He was *looking* and **LISTENING** for any sign of movement. But nothing came.

'It's getting close to the end of the match,' Lise said, glancing down at her watch. Maybe we should . . .'

'Pack up? Yeah, maybe,' Marcus said. He ground his teeth in frustration. 'Let's pack everything away.'

Stacey sighed, but nodded her head in agreement. Asim started to walk towards the sheet, but just as he'd taken his first step, something happened.

Marcus was suddenly aware that the entire hallway had gone silent. Even the sounds of the basketball game next door seemed to have disappeared.

Then he heard it. Footsteps.

Dread crept up his spine. The hairs on his neck were standing on end. Next to him, Lise clenched her fists.

Very slowly, Marcus turned around.

It was the Ghoul.

Chapter Eleven

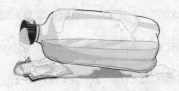

The clouds outside suddenly shifted, casting the hallway into unnatural shadow.

Even though this is what the Breakfast Club Investigators had hoped for, Marcus had forgotten how terrifying the Ghoul was. How it cast an aura over everything around it, **wrapping the hallway in darkness.**

Marcus's mouth fell open. Everything

felt tight. It was like someone had wrapped a bunch of **giant rubber bands** around his chest. He couldn't move. But on the inside, his stomach was *churning*.

Ahead, the Ghoul started to slowly walk down the corridor, making those horribly ominous footsteps. It let out its **terrible groan**, which tore at Marcus's mind.

The Ghoul reared back suddenly, and then reached out with its arms and started moving forward even more quickly.

It was halfway down the corridor now, creeping ever closer to the Investigators with its loud, booming footsteps.

But they weren't the only thing it was close to.

'The sheet!' Marcus yelped, pointing right at it with a shaking arm. 'We need to trap it with the sheet!'

'Yes!' Stacey exclaimed. Her lip trembled. 'You go.'

'No, you go.' Marcus shot her a scared look.

The Ghoul inched closer.

'I'm definitely not going,' Asim whispered, taking a step behind Marcus.

'What if **all of us** go, all at once?' Lise said. Her eyes were screwed tightly together.

Marcus swallowed. He tried to think but his mind was blank.

The Ghoul came closer still.

Stacey cried, 'Now!' and, as one, the Breakfast Club Investigators rushed down the corridor. Four pairs of feet moving together. Towards the rope. Towards the sheet. Towards the Ghoul.

As soon as he was within reach, Marcus reached up and pulled **HARD** on the rope.

But nothing happened. The sheet should have **swooped** down onto the Ghoul and trapped it. What was going on?

He yanked it again and again, but nothing changed. The rope must have got caught on something.

'Come on!' Stacey yelled.

'It's getting closer! It's getting *too* close!' Asim shouted.

Marcus pulled again, as hard as he could, and finally the sheet moved. It shot up to the ceiling, the force causing it to *flip around,* and then it **swooped down** and landed on the Breakfast Club Investigators.

They stumbled back, crashing over each other and onto the floor.

The sheet was completely wrapped all around them. **None of the group could see anything.**

'We need to get up,' Stacey exclaimed.

'Are those footsteps? Can you still hear the Ghoul's footsteps?' Marcus shouted.

'Did we get eaten by the Ghoul?!' Asim cried.

'We need to move, now!' Stacey said again, louder this time.

Stacey and Lise tried to stand up, while Asim and Marcus tried to get to their knees. They **PULLED** the sheet in different directions, dragging each other this way and that. Once they were all on their feet, they ran as fast as they could, still completely covered in the sheet.

Marcus didn't know where they were going, he just knew they had to get as far away from the Ghoul as possible.

With a painful yelp they crashed into a wall, but then they were running forward, down the corridor. Marcus just hoped it was away from the Ghoul.

He could just make out a steady thump coming from up ahead. Panicked, he thought for one wild second that the Ghoul had gotten ahead of them, but before he could stop they suddenly tumbled forwards through a door.

There was a ripple of *gasps*. Before Marcus could even stop to think about where they were, his foot hit something large and round, and he staggered forward, pulling everyone else down with him. They thudded into someone and then crashed onto the floor in a painful heap.

Then he heard footsteps coming straight for them. But these footsteps were not the loud, heavy footsteps of the Ghoul.

The sheet was ripped off the group. Marcus blinked as bright lights hit his eyes.

His stomach **dropped** as he realized where they were — in the centre of the basketball court in the gym. The referee was right next to them, grimacing and rubbing his ankle.

'What on earth are you doing?' a very **angry** Mrs Miller asked as she glared down at them.

Chapter Twelve

TICK.
 TOCK.

Marcus stared directly at the clock. He followed the second hand as it slowly eased around. It was going so slowly that Marcus wondered if it was even moving at all.

TICK.
TOCK.

'First of all,' Stacey said quickly, 'I just

wanted to say sorry—'

Mrs Miller raised a hand to cut her off. 'I don't want to hear your excuses, Miss To.' she said.

Marcus glanced down from the clock. The Breakfast Club Investigators were stood in Mrs Miller's small office, in a line in front of her desk. Their head teacher was sat down in on the other side. She was looking extremely serious.

This wasn't the first time the BCI had been here, but it felt different today.

'You interrupted an intraschool basketball game.' Mrs Miller was shaking her head. 'The referee rolled his ankle after you crashed into him. He couldn't continue, so they had to abandon the match! Do you know how **embarrassing** that is for our school?

You are not children any more.'

'I know. We're sorry, Mrs Miller, but we did it because we were following a lead in an investigation – we know it was bad, but—'

Mrs Miller cut Stacey off again. 'I spoke to Gbenga. You've been talking about some **curse,** and **ghosts.** The team's already struggling, and you four getting involved doesn't help the situation.'

'But the Ghoul–'

'I don't want to hear another word about ghosts or ghouls,' Mrs Miller said loudly. She leaned back in her chair, shaking her head once more. She took a deep breath. 'I love clubs as much as anyone at this school, but it's my job to make sure all clubs have the opportunity to thrive, not just the Breakfast Club Investigators. This amount of chaos is just too much. I know it's sad, but, unfortunately, **I think the Breakfast Club Investigators experiment has run its course.** Don't you think?' she said, gazing at each of the group in turn.

It felt like a trapdoor had just opened underneath Marcus, and now he was falling. The words tumbled out of his mouth. 'But you can't!'

This was how it happened. The group falls apart, and then they stop hanging out with each other. They lose each other.

'I have to,' Mrs Miller said firmly.

Marcus hung his head. He knew that there was no point in arguing.

Asim kept opening his mouth like he had something to say, but nothing came out. Lise just stared straight ahead with glazed eyes.

Then Stacey said the dreaded words. 'OK, the Breakfast Club Investigators are over.' She spoke quickly, like she didn't want the words in her mouth any longer than they had to be.

Mrs Miller nodded her approval. 'Good. You each have a **detention** after school today and I'll be keeping an eye on you all from now on.' She pointed at each of them in turn. 'This time, we didn't have to make any calls home. But if this goes any further, I will have to get your parents involved.'

Marcus swallowed hard. He did not want a call home to his mum, not under any circumstances.

'Am I making myself clear?' Mrs Miller asked sternly.

'Yes, Mrs Miller,' they said together.

And with that, Mrs Miller dismissed them from her office with a wave of her hand.

Marcus hung his head and trudged out after the other Investigators. His body was on autopilot as he took slow steps down the hallway.

Did that really just happen?

As soon as they were out of earshot of Mrs Miller's office, he turned to Stacey. 'Stacey,' Marcus mumbled. She didn't respond. 'Stacey!' Marcus reached over and touched her shoulder. Stacey turned around and shushed him.

'Wait,' she whispered.

Stacey **tiptoed** down the corridor, glancing into classrooms until she found one she liked the look of.

'This one is empty.' She beckoned to the

rest of the group, and Marcus, Lise and Asim crept into the classroom behind her.

Marcus slumped into a chair. Thoughts were rushing around his head, moving so fast that it took an effort to get the words out. 'You just ended it. Us. Just like that,' he said.

Stacey turned to him with a **surprised** look on her face. 'Who do you think I am? Of course I didn't! Do you really think I'm going to give up just because our head teacher told us to stop?' she asked. The pit in Marcus's stomach got just a little bit **smaller.**

'Well, maybe . . .' Marcus admitted, scratching his chin. He felt a little silly now. He turned to Lise and Asim. 'Was I the only one who thought that Stacey was actually breaking us up?'

'No, I totally thought the Breakfast Club

142

Investigators were done-zo,' Asim said.

'Done-zo?' Marcus's eyebrows shot up.

Asim groaned. 'When I'm stressed I say words I don't normally say, OK?' He wiped a thin film of sweat off his forehead.

'Stacey is obsessed with mysteries,' Lise added. 'There's no way she would just quit them.' She grinned at Stacey.

'Well, that's not completely wrong,' Stacey said mischievously. 'I *had* to say we were breaking up the group. That's the only way we could get Mrs Miller off our backs! Listen, we'll talk about this properly after school at detention.'

Marcus nodded, feeling a tiny bit better.

After school, the Breakfast Club Investigators slowly moped around the gym, picking up empty packets of crisps and sweet wrappers and putting them into bin bags. Mrs Miller had decided their detention should be spent cleaning up after the basketball match.

Across the gym, Mr Anderson was sitting reading a book.

Marcus stopped and glanced around, wiping a hand across his forehead. They were only halfway through, and they'd been here for around an hour. It was incredibly dull work. He sighed and tried to take a step, but his foot felt like it was **STUCK** to the floor.

'I think that's gum,' Lise said, pointing at his shoe.

Marcus groaned.

'I've got the gum scraper,' Stacey said, waving a metal scraper in her hand.

'I'll help,' Asim said.

They all came over
to where Marcus was
standing. Asim
and Lise lifted
his leg

while Stacey scraped the gum off his shoe.

'**No talking!**' Mr Anderson called out from across the room.

'We're not, we're just helping Marcus with gum on his shoe,' Stacey called back.

They stood around next to each other, silent for a moment, and then Marcus whispered. 'So, what now?'

'I think we need to regroup,' Lise said. 'Not much has gone well so far.'

'Are you talking about the part where we didn't catch the Ghoul, or the part where Mrs Miller disbanded the BCI?' Asim huffed.

'All of it, really,' Lise replied grimly.

Mr Anderson's voice came floating towards them. 'That's still too much talking.'

The group fell silent, and went back to cleaning.

A few minutes later, Marcus spotted something **SHINY** on the floor in the corner of the gym. He walked towards it, thinking it was just another piece of rubbish. But as he approached, he realized that it was one of the badges that the Journalism Club wore. What's more, it was underneath a bottle.

Marcus reached and picked up both objects. The bottle was sticky, and seemed to be filled with a **thick liquid.** Marcus frowned at it – he was sure he'd seen this liquid before . . .

Then it hit him. He'd seen it on the

basketball club jerseys that Gbenga had showed them. It was *ectoplasm*.

Marcus opened the bottle and peered more closely at the liquid. Up close, it looked and smelled like some kind of **watery jelly.**

Marcus glanced around the room, lightly coughing until Stacey, Lise and Asim turn to look at him.

'I think I've found something,' Marcus hissed.

'What is it?' Stacey slowly crept to his side,

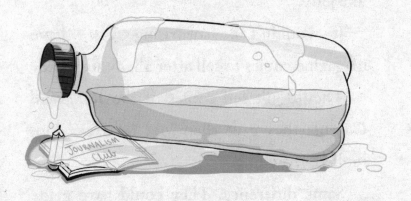

keeping an eye on Mr Anderson. The others quickly followed.

Asim gasped when he saw what Marcus was holding. 'Journalism Club!' he murmured furiously.

'They have ectoplasm!' Stacey whispered. 'They're working with the Ghoul!'

'Or they *are* the Ghoul . . .' Marcus said slowly. 'Think about it. It makes sense! What if they made up the whole story with the Ghoul? And this ectoplasm actually looks like jelly.'

'It wouldn't be surprising. They have magazine copies to sell after all,' Stacey said.

'They don't sell copies of the *Rutherford Gazette*; they give them out for free,' Lise replied, frowning.

'Same difference. They could have made

everything up just to get *attention*,' Marcus said.

'Are you sure about this?' Lise looked down at her feet.

'Positive. They just want attention. They don't care about mysteries like we do,' Marcus said.

'It's the **perfect crime.** A crime only *they* can solve because *they're* the criminals!' Asim said.

'Let's not jump to any conclusions,' Lise said. 'Sure, it's suspicious and I'm not saying it doesn't need investigating, but there could still be a Ghoul.'

'Are you still talking?' Mr Anderson's voice **rang** through the room. The group scattered again.

After another half an hour or so, detention

was over. As Marcus, Stacey, Asim and Lise trudged after Mr Anderson, they heard a voice calling out to them. It was Georgina.

'Gbenga's offered to drop the case. If you want to stop investigating, you're welcome to,' she said. It was like she'd appeared out of nowhere.

Marcus glanced ahead of him, but Mr Anderson had already disappeared down the hallway. 'What do you mean, offered to drop the case?' he asked.

'He's giving you an easy way out, now that you're **banned**,' Georgina replied.

'How do you know we're banned?' Stacey asked.

Georgina looked at her through narrowed eyes. '*Everyone* knows. The whole school saw what you did! And news travels here.'

'I kinda already figured that out,' Asim muttered under his breath.

'We've already decided. **We're still investigating**,' Stacey said firmly.

'Are you sure?' Georgina asked.

'Yes,' Lise said emphatically.

'Fine, but the offer's always open. Anyway, I've got to go – I don't want to be around this gym after dark any longer than I have to.' And with a wave of her hand, Georgina walked off.

Something about the encounter was weird, but Marcus couldn't put his finger on it.

'Why doesn't Gbenga give the case to the Journalism Club?' Marcus asked slowly, as the four of them hurried to catch up to Mr Anderson.

'Maybe he believes in us?' Lise said uncertainly. 'That if we can't solve it, no one can?'

'And knows that they're just **CASE STEALERS**,' Stacey added.

There was a pause, and then Marcus said, 'Yeah, maybe . . .' He glanced back at the closed doors of the gym, thinking hard.

Chapter Thirteen

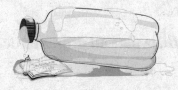

'We should be investigating the Journalism Club right now,' Marcus hissed over the table at Breakfast Club the next day. Mr Anderson still let them sit together even though technically they were broken up as a club. 'And we should be asking them why one of their badges was left next to a bottle of ectoplasm, or jelly, or whatever it was that was on that basketball uniform! Why are we waiting?'

'We just need to lay low a little bit. We're still going to do it today, just later,' Stacey responded. 'We can't risk getting caught by Mrs Miller.'

'Yeah, relax, it's all going to be fine,' Asim said.

'I *am* relaxed, maybe you're the one who's not relaxed!' Marcus responded angrily.

'I'm so relaxed that I could take a nap, like right now!' Asim shot back.

'Doesn't look like that to me,' Marcus snapped.

'Please stop!' Lise exclaimed. 'We're all on the same team.'

'Look, let's just meet outside the English classrooms after school, and then we can investigate the Journalism Club properly,' Stacey insisted.

Marcus grunted his agreement. He glanced away from them, tapping his foot rapidly. He could see other people at Breakfast Club sneaking glances at his group and **sniggering.** Their reputation had been ruined. They had to fix this.

At lunchtime, Marcus ignored Oyin and Patrick's calls as he passed the football pitch. He wanted to be alone, to give himself some **space** to think.

He ended up sitting down at the foot of one of the staircases outside a maths classroom. His mind was racing, thinking about everything that had happened in the past week. He put his head in his hands.

'What's up?' a voice asked from above. Marcus looked up. It was Gbenga.

'Oh, hi Gbenga,' said Marcus in a gloomy voice. 'I'm just thinking about our investigation . . .'

'Do you want to talk about it?' Gbenga asked.

'It's – well, it's the others – they just don't understand. No one really understands,' he finished under his breath.

Gbenga sat down next to him. 'Why don't you try me?'

Marcus heaved a **MASSIVE** sigh. 'It's just . . . we're going to break up for real this time. The others don't see it yet, but the Breakfast Club Investigators won't last if we keep going like this.'

Gbenga shot him a sideways glance. 'Are you talking about the fact that you haven't been able to solve the mystery, or that the group is banned?'

Marcus took a deep breath. 'Both,' he admitted. Then he buried his face in his hands again. 'This is our *last chance,* and they're acting like – like –' Marcus couldn't find the words.

'Like everything's normal?' Gbenga suggested.

Marcus had the feeling that Gbenga understood exactly what he was going through. 'Yeah, like it's all normal . . . But they don't get it – we can only be investigators because other kids believe in us and bring us their cases,' Marcus said. 'If they stop because the Journalism Club becomes the place to go if you have a mystery, then . . .' he trailed off miserably.

'The Breakfast Club Investigators wouldn't exist any more,' Gbenga finished for him.

'Right,' Marcus said, biting his lip.

'Of course they don't understand. They're not like us,' Gbenga said, shaking his head. Marcus shot him a quizzical look. 'I'm the captain of the basketball team, so whenever something goes wrong all eyes are on me.

The whole school just expects me to be good enough to overcome anything, but if they saw how hard I have to work and that being good didn't all come to me naturally, then . . . Then – they wouldn't be here. But that's just how it is . . .' Gbenga said sadly.

Marcus frowned, thinking. 'But that's **NOT FAIR**.' he said. He was talking about Gbenga, but thinking about himself and the Breakfast Club Investigators. It was the same there; people just expected them to solve everything quickly and easy.

'It's not fair,' Gbenga agreed, 'but that's how it is for both of us.'

'Yeah, for both of us,' Marcus said. It felt nice to talk to someone who understood what he was going through.

The bell *rang*, signalling the end of lunch.

'Thanks for just talking with me,' Marcus said, suddenly feeling awkward.

'No worries. It felt good for me to talk about this too.' Gbenga smiled. 'Just let me know if you ever want to have a talk again.'

Marcus smiled back, before they both left for class.

Chapter Fourteen

At the end of the school day, The Breakfast Club Investigators waited outside the English classrooms.

While Asim kept watch, Marcus, Stacey and Lise **crouched** close to the ground, making sure to keep out of sight. Peering through the windows, they could see that Maxine and Noah were hovering around a printer along with four other kids Marcus didn't know. Great big stacks of paper and

wooden stands were laid out all around the room.

Marcus kept his eyes squarely trained through the window. 'It looks like something's happening,' he said after a couple of minutes.

Noah had retrieved something from a desk and handed it to Maxine. It was a brownish piece of paper in a plastic wallet. Maxine read what was on the paper, and her eyes went **wide.**

'It looks like a **really, really old** piece of paper,' Lise said, scrunching her nose.

'It looks like something that could have a spell on it,' Stacey said eagerly. 'Maybe it's something that could summon a Ghoul!'

'Either way, it's a clue,' Lise said.

Maxine said something to Noah.

'What are they saying?' Marcus said. It was hard for him to hear them from here.

Asim squinted through the glass, trying to read Maxine's lips. 'I think she said something about the **RUTHERFORD RHYMERS,**' he said finally.

Stacey scrunched up her nose. 'The Rutherford Rhymers? I didn't know we had a rap group at school. I think that might be wrong, Asim.'

Asim thought for a moment. 'Maybe it was the **Rutherford Rainbows?**' he suggested.

'What does that even mean?' Stacey hissed.

Marcus squinted, trying his best to ignore the sounds of their squabbling.

Then it clicked.

'The Rutherford Rhinos!' Marcus whispered loudly. 'I think that's what Maxine said.'

'What does *that* mean?' Asim asked.

'I think that's what Rutherford's basketball team used to be called years ago,' Marcus said slowly. 'Someone in football club told me ages ago. But they dropped the name long before we joined.'

'Wait . . . didn't Georgina mention something about them?' Stacey said, frowning.

Lise nodded excitedly. 'Yes, I think so! She said that the school basketball team had been cursed by a Ghoul years ago!'

'She must have been talking about the Rutherford Rhinos then!' Asim added.

Marcus looked at Asim. Something was wrong here.

'Wait, who's keeping a lookout?' Marcus exclaimed, looking left and then right.

Suddenly, they heard footsteps coming from down the hall. For a split second Marcus thought it was the Ghoul, but then he realized they belonged to something else. Something just as terrifying.

'Teachers!' Stacey hissed.

Without another word, the group scattered. Marcus **rushed** down the hallway and then **CLATTERED** down the stairs. He tore through the doors and across the car park, not stopping until he was back at the hideout. Doubled over, trying to catch his breath, he realized that he was alone. He'd lost the rest of his group in the chaos of their escape.

One by one, Stacey, Lise and Asim arrived, looking just as out of breath as Marcus. They all slumped on the sofa, panting.

After a few minutes, Stacey stood up once more. 'The Rutherford Rhinos,' she said triumphantly. '*That's* what the Journalism Club were talking about!'

She was standing in front of the board with the sketch of the Ghoul on it, holding her notebook.

Suddenly, Georgina's words came back to Marcus.

There are rumours. Rumours that something went wrong with Rutherford basketball team in the past. They were cursed by something.

'The old basketball team,' Marcus muttered. A thought flashed across his mind. 'It makes sense.' He stood up to join Stacey. 'Something must have happened with the school basketball team in the past.'

'And that's why the team is cursed now,' Stacey said loudly.

'So, are you saying we just need to figure out what happened?' Lise asked.

'That won't be easy,' Asim looked worried. They were all silent for a moment, thinking about the task that lay ahead of them.

'But . . . maybe it is.' Lise looked like she was choosing her words carefully. 'Where's the place you go if you need information about things?' she asked.

'My dad,' Asim said immediately.

'This book.' Stacey held up her book on the supernatural.

'My mum,' Marcus said.

'No!' Lise threw up her arms. **I'm talking about the library!** We just need to go to the school library. They have a ton of books and even an archive of old school newspapers. Maybe we can find something about the Rutherford Rhinos there.'

'Oh, yeah!' said Stacey. 'Great idea, Lise! But we'll have to do it tomorrow during lunchtime. My parents won't be happy if I'm home late *again*.'

Marcus had a reading hour with his mum tonight, and he didn't want to let her down.

'Agreed,' he said. 'Let's meet again tomorrow lunchtime in the library.'

The others nodded.

Stacey beamed at them all. 'Good work today, gang,' she said. *We're onto something* – I just *know* we're getting close to solving this case, and finding out what the Journalism Club are up to.'

Chapter Fifteen

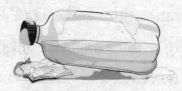

The next day was Wednesday, which meant that the Breakfast Club Investigators only had **two days** to solve the mystery before the basketball tournament started.

Marcus, Stacey, Lise and Asim walked into the library at lunchtime.

'What are you doing here?' a familiar voice said. Marcus froze and looked up. It was Mr Anderson.

He sighed. 'I'm going to pretend I didn't see you.' Shaking his head, he gave them all a warning glance and then left the library.

'We are so lucky. We are so *so* lucky,' Marcus breathed as they walked towards the rows and rows of bookshelves **crammed** into the small room.

Wordlessly, they looked around to make sure that no other teachers were there, before Lise led them over to the very back of the library. In a *forgotten, dusty corner*, tons of boxes were stacked on top of one another, crammed full of school newspapers.

'I think I remember how this is organized,' Lise muttered as she bent down and began to flick through them. 'Give me a second, and then I should be able to find the archived ones.'

'While we're here, we might as well do a

little book returning,' Stacey said, slipping her backpack off. She walked to the book deposit. Marcus and Asim followed.

'What do you have?' Marcus asked.

With a rueful smile, Stacey lifted the book to the light.

'*The Forgotten Pen*.' Asim read the title of the book aloud.

'It's the third book in this mystery series

by H. S. Brimley. It's . . . well, it's about a group of kids who solve mysteries,' Stacey said, a little awkwardly.

'It looks cool!' Marcus said.

Stacey beamed at him.

'So, that's where you got the idea of the club from,' Asim said. 'Actually, I need to put mine back too. It's a graphic novel, one of the Asterix and Obelix ones. Have you read

them?' he asked eagerly, lifting up the comic.

'No,' said Marcus and Stacey in unison.

'They drink **magic** potions and **smash** Ancient Romans! It's fun, and the drawings are very cool,' Asim went on excitedly.

'What about you, Marcus?' Stacey said.

'I'm reading *Salamander and the Memory Magicians*. It's fantasy. I like it, but I haven't finished it yet,' Marcus replied. Then he suddenly smiled at the other two. 'Hey, we should start a **book club**!'

'Yeah!' said Asim. 'I had no idea you guys were into books.'

'Me neither,' Stacey grinned.

Suddenly, Lise's voice floated towards them over the shelves. 'Guys, I think I found something.'

Marcus, Asim and Stacey hurried back over

to where Lise was. She was sitting on the floor surrounded by newspapers. In front of her was a plastic wallet filled with some cuttings.

'What is that?' Marcus said, leaning over her. The paper in the plastic wallet looked **brown, dry and crumbly.**

'Just be careful! It's very **fragile,**' Lise said. 'They're old student newspapers. Here they're writing about the school's first basketball team. The Rutherford Rhinos.' There was excitement coursing through Lise's voice. 'They were good. Apparently so good that they won a whole bunch of tournaments all over the country.' Lise pointed to a grainy photo of a team lifting a trophy. 'But then things went wrong.'

'What happened?' Stacey said, leaning in. She was hanging onto Lise's every word.

'There was a leadership struggle. The captain ended up being replaced, and he didn't like that.' Lise turned the paper around. Now they were looking at the front page.

'CURSED', was the headline.

'He cursed the team,' Marcus breathed. Asim let out a sharp **gasp.**

Stacey straightened up. 'Well, we just need to find a way to lift that curse.'

'Or . . .' Marcus began hesitantly, 'what if the curse is just an excuse for the Journalism Club to spin this tale about a Ghoul so they can beat us.' He bit his lip.

'We shouldn't talk about it here,' said Lise. 'We might get caught by a teacher – let's go to the hideout.'

The moment they stepped out of the library, Marcus saw a hint of movement from his left-hand side. He flinched.

'What's up?' Asim said from behind him. Marcus didn't answer.

'Who's there?' he called out. He was looking to where the hallway turned a corner. 'Show yourself!' **His heart began to thump in his chest.**

Two people stepped out from around the corner.

It was Maxine and Noah.

'What are *you* doing here?' Stacey said rudely.

'I could ask you the same thing,' Maxine shot back.

Marcus couldn't help but find something off about this.

'Wait . . . were you following us?' he asked incredulously.

'I don't know what you're talking about,' Maxine replied, raising an eyebrow.

'You *were* following us!' Marcus shouted, pointing at them.

'That's not cool, Maxine,' Lise mumbled.

'You were all following us first! You think we didn't see you **creeping** around outside our room last night?' Maxine said fiercely.

'That's because we don't trust you,' Marcus said.

'Yeah, we found a pin of yours next to a bottle of ectoplasm. The very same ectoplasm that was on basketball uniforms attacked by the Ghoul!' Stacey said.

'Er, I think it was jelly,' Marcus said. 'But the point still stands! You pretended to be—'

'You summoned—' Stacey interjected.

'THE GHOUL,' they both said together.

Noah gave a wry smile. He bent down and whispered something to Maxine.

'What's Noah saying? Why doesn't he just tell us?' Marcus said, his frustration rising.

'Noah said that you're trying to frame us for the Ghoul, because we worked on some mysteries that you couldn't solve,' Maxine said, crossing her arms over her chest. 'And I think he's right.'

Lise looked uncomfortably from Maxine and Noah to Stacey and Marcus. 'Maybe we need to just talk about this,' she said anxiously.

'I have nothing to talk about,' Marcus said. He **scowled** at Noah.

'And that's why you won't solve any more cases,' Maxine said lightly. She smirked.

'What do you mean?' Marcus said. He'd had enough of this. 'What does she mean?'

No one responded.

'You know, if we really were so evil and out to get you then we would just report you to Mrs Miller,' Maxine said. *Marcus's heart sank.* 'But,' she went on, 'we're not going to do that. But we *are* going to solve this case before you.' And with that, she turned and walked away, Noah following after.

Chapter Sixteen

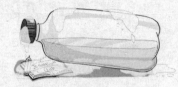

At the hideout that evening, the four of them sat in silence. Asim was by the window, gazing absentmindedly out of it. Stacey was poring over her book of the supernatural in the corner. Marcus and Lise sat on opposite ends of the couch, their minds elsewhere.

'It feels like we're getting somewhere,' Lise said finally. 'But the thing is, we now have less than two days to crack this.' She looked concerned.

'I feel like we know so much, but not enough,' Marcus muttered.

'We're close, **we just have to push a little bit more**,' Stacey said. She rubbed her chin. 'Let's go over what we know about the case.'

'Well, the Basketball Club is **cursed**.' Asim shrugged. 'And it looks like they got cursed years ago by the captain of the team back then.'

'Maybe the curse disappeared for a while and then came back – curses can do that, you know,' said Stacey thoughtfully.

'It explains everything – why they suddenly started playing bad, and why the Ghoul is *haunting* them,' Lise said, ticking each point off on her fingers.

'But it doesn't explain how we solve this case,' Marcus said. He put his head in his hands.

'To do that we have to figure out how to lift the curse,' Stacey said.

'Maybe we have to face the Ghoul and defeat it,' Asim said with a **shiver.**

'Maybe we could talk to the Ghoul, get it to see that what it's doing isn't exactly the best thing for the school,' Lise suggested.

Marcus shook his head. 'I'm not sure Ghouls are up for negotiations, Lise.'

'Well, do you have any ideas?' she said sharply.

'No, not really, but I'm sure we'll come up with something. We just need to think.' Marcus said.

There was quiet as everyone thought hard.

'What about Maxine?' Stacey said suddenly.

'What *about* Maxine?' Marcus's eyes narrowed.

'I mean, she said there's a reason thatthe Journalism Club solve more mysteries than us. Maybe there's something she knows about us or the mystery that could help us solve this.'

'Well, if it helps us solve the mys—' Lise started.

'*No*,' Marcus interrupted. 'We can't work with them. *We* can solve this! We have to!' He **refused** to ask the Journalism Club for help.

'I don't know if we can,' Asim said in a shaky voice.

Marcus turned to look at him. Asim looked

so pale, it was like all the blood had run out of his face. He was still looking out of the window, his eyes glued to something in the distance.

With **dread** slowly creeping up his spine, Marcus got up and walked nervously to where Asim was. He peered out of the window.

It was getting late, and the evening's gloom

had begun to creep out of dark corners, taking hold of the space outside the hideout. Dark enough to scrub detail away from the outside world. But in the distance, Marcus could just make out something moving.

A shadowy figure standing at the far end of the teachers' car park.

'The Ghoul!' Marcus cried as he stumbled back from the window, falling onto his bottom. 'It's coming for us!'

Chapter Seventeen

'What?' yelped Stacey as she and Lise hurried to the window. They both gasped as they saw the shadowy figure.

'Get down,' Lise said urgently, pulling Marcus and Stacey to the floor. Asim, broken out of his reverie, quickly followed suit – it was like Marcus's yell had shocked him into action. The four of them crouched below the window, wide-eyed.

'What if, because we're investigating the Ghoul, its curse will go onto us as well?' Stacey whispered. She looked panicked.

'Now is not the time for theories, Stacey,' Lise whispered back. Her hands were covering her eyes.

A minute passed. And then another. Marcus hoped against hope that the Ghoul had just gone away, left them alone.

But then came the sound he had been dreading: footsteps. **Deep and heavy, they echoed around the hideout.** Marcus's eyes darted around desperately, but he knew there was **NO ESCAPE** except for the door, which the Ghoul was heading for. They were trapped.

The footsteps were close now, so *so* close.

Marcus shut his eyes tight, expecting at

any moment to hear the slow, high-pitched squeak of the hideout door opening.

And then the footsteps stopped.

Marcus strained his ears, but he couldn't hear anything. He opened his eyes. But he didn't dare voice the thought that was on his mind.

Has it gone?

'One of us should probably check the door,' Asim whispered eventually. 'Right? I mean, not me, but someone should do it.'

Marcus took a deep breath. 'I'll do it.' He steeled himself, and then crawled along the floor, inch by inch, until he reached the door. He slowly edged his way up, his heart **pounding** with every move he made, until he could reach the door handle. He took one last deep breath, and then turned it. The door creaked open with a *rusty squeak.* Marcus quickly stuck his head outside.

'Is the Ghoul there?' Asim squeaked.

Marcus shook his head slowly. The car park looked empty; the Ghoul was nowhere to be seen.

'IT'S GONE.' Marcus sighed with relief. He got to his feet. It was then that he noticed something outside on the ground, just past the threshold of the door.

He stared at it for a moment, trying to

make it out. And then it hit him – with a **sinking dread,** he realized what it was.

Marcus called back to Stacey, Lise and Asim, 'You need to see this.'

His friends came over to where he stood.

In front of them, on the floor, was a splash of **rubbery liquid.**

'It left something behind,' Lise said darkly.

'A mark,' Stacey added. 'Its **ectoplasm.**'

Next to her, Asim was taking big gulping breaths. He began to talk really fast, 'It marked our hideout with ectoplasm? What if we're cursed now and haunted and followed by the Ghoul wherever we go and—'

Stacey grabbed Asim's shoulders.

'Don't worry. There's nothing we can do now. I'm sure it's nothing.' She took a deep breath, but that glint in her eye was back. 'I think it's time we went home anyway. We've made great progress today, and tomorrow we can figure out what the Ghoul leaving its ectoplasm here might mean. *We're so close*, I can feel it.'

Chapter Eighteen

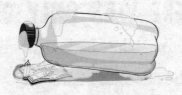

The next morning, Marcus was kicking a ball around in the playground with Oyin and Patrick on their way to Breakfast Club.

Oyin passed the ball to Patrick.

Marcus couldn't stop thinking about the Ghoul. **Was the BCI really cursed too? Is that why the ectoplasm showed up?**

Patrick kicked the ball back to Oyin.

All Marcus knew for sure was that time was running out. If they wanted to solve this case, then they had to find a way to do it right now. **THERE WAS ONLY ONE DAY LEFT** before the basketball tournament started. They couldn't fail.

Oyin kicked the ball to Marcus.

Marcus tried to control the ball, but it all

went wrong. The ball **slipped** away from his foot at an odd angle. He tried to juggle the ball with his feet, but it immediately fell to the floor and **bounced away** sadly.

Marcus groaned.

'What just happened?' Oyin asked.

'Marcus? That was so unlike you,' Patrick added.

Marcus frowned. 'I don't know,' he

said slowly. He went to retrieve the ball and attempted to pass it to Patrick, but he misjudged it. Badly.

Marcus stopped dead. What was happening?

'Marcus,' Oyin began hesitantly, 'has something happened to your touch again?'

Marcus gaped at her, his heart beating fast. 'It-it can't have,' he whispered. *His mind was racing.* A couple of months ago he had lost his touch, after he lost his cousin's football. It had come back then, but would it come back now? 'I've got to *run* – see you guys later.' And with that he tore towards Breakfast Club, not stopping until he reached the table under the noisy air conditioner. He was relieved to see that Stacey, Lise and Asim were all sitting there, eating cereal.

'Has something gone wrong with you? Anything?' he panted, the moment he reached the table.

Stacey lifted her head up, she had been searching through her backpack.

'Well, I seem to have lost my book on the supernatural. Don't worry, though, I should be able to find it soon,' she said with a tired-looking grin. 'It's not in the hideout or in my backpack or at home.'

'That's **weird**, last night, when I was trying to paint, I kept mixing all my paints into the wrong colours . . .' Asim said. 'I couldn't seem to get anything right!'

'Now you mention it . . .' Lise began hesitantly, 'I couldn't concentrate when I was trying to read last night. My mind kept **drifting away.** It hasn't happened before

– usually I get lost in the book.'

Marcus felt a **pit of worry** start to form in his stomach. 'And I've lost my touch again. I think we might be . . .' Marcus trailed off, unsure how to finish.

Stacey's eyes widened. *'Are we cursed?'* she exclaimed. They all stared at each other uncertainly.

'But how do we stop it?!' Asim said desperately. 'I'm working on a new painting for Art Club, we have an exhibition coming up soon! I can't just not paint!'

'I'm working on a new engineering project, and I need to finish my research for it,' Lise cried.

'I have a school football match next week. I can't lose my touch again, I need to be on the team!' Marcus said. It was all starting to sink in. He remembered how **horrible** it was last time he lost his touch. He couldn't let it happen again.

'We have to find a way to lift the curse!' Lise said with a shiver.

Stacey put her hands on the table and took a deep breath. 'Maybe,' she began hesitantly, 'it's time to talk to the Journalism Club and find out what they know.' It looked like she had struggled to even say the words.

'Absolutely not,' Marcus said immediately. 'We found their badge with the bottle of jelly. They're involved with this.'

'Then maybe that's a reason to talk to them,' Stacey said hotly. 'Maybe **they summoned the Ghoul** and then lost control of it? Maybe a million things happened! There's just no way we'll find out without talking to them.'

'Talk to them?' Marcus cried. He felt his temper rising. 'It's not just the Basketball Club that got hurt here. We're **cursed** too now, remember? If they summoned the Ghoul then, technically, they cursed *us*!'

'Maybe you're right, but even if you *are* right we still need to talk to them. What else can we do?' Stacey said.

They both looked over at Asim.

'I vote to talk to them,' he said. 'They're not that bad.'

Marcus glared at him. 'It's **dangerous**,' he said.

'Everything we do now is dangerous. First, we were banned by Mrs Miller, and now we're cursed.' Stacey chuckled.

'We don't need their help. We're the

Breakfast Club Investigators,' Marcus said. He looked around the **vibrant, buzzing** Breakfast Club, thinking about how it had brought them together.

'And we'll still be the same Breakfast Club Investigators after we talk to them,' Stacey said sharply. Marcus could tell he was starting to get on their nerves, but he didn't care.

'Will we? Who's going to come to us for help if we need someone else to solve our cases?' Marcus said. His face felt **HOT,** and he felt like the words were falling out of his mouth before he could form them properly. 'We're the helpers. If we need help, then what's the point of any of it?' No one else replied. The only sound at the table was Marcus's heavy breathing.

'Maybe we should take a break and talk about this tomorrow,' Asim said quietly.

'We don't have time to take a break. The tournament starts *tomorrow*. We have one day left, and you're going to let us ruin it.' And with that, Marcus turned on his heel and **stormed out** of the canteen.

He walked quickly through the school's empty hallways, bumping into kids, not caring where he was going, until he **crashed** into someone so hard that he fell to the floor with an **'Oof!'**

'Marcus, is that you?' The voice was coming from above him. Marcus looked up to see Gbenga's face peering down at him with concern.

'Oh, hi Gbenga,' Marcus said quietly.

Gbenga held out a hand, which Marcus

gratefully took, and Gbenga pulled him to his feet.

'Are you OK?' Gbenga asked.

Marcus glanced up at him, and couldn't stop himself from **EXPLODING.** 'They want us to ask for help! They want us to go to the Journalism Club and work with them!'

Gbenga seemed to know what he was talking about straight away. 'They really don't understand, do they?' he said. There was a sad look on his face, like he had known all along that this would happen.

'No, they don't,' Marcus replied sulkily. 'If we ask for help, we'll lose everything. **The Breakfast Club Investigators won't exist** when everyone knows we just get help from the Journalism Club. No one will bring us cases.'

'Of course they won't. They want us to be naturally good, to be able to just succeed at everything,' Gbenga said, scowling.

Marcus sank down onto the floor of the corridor. He felt exhausted.

'What if we can't?' Marcus asked. 'We've already been **BANNED** by Mrs Miller. Maybe there's no point in the club carrying on any more . . .'

'You have to.' Gbenga's eyes were suddenly very intense. He reached out and placed a hand on Marcus's shoulder. 'Listen, you have to do whatever it takes to protect the club.'

'Whatever it takes?' Marcus repeated.

'Whatever it takes. Even if things go in a way you didn't expect. If they go in a way you can't control. Even then it's worth it.'

'Really?' Marcus felt confused. He thought

Gbenga was a **hero** – he was a legend around school, after all – but there was something odd about what he was saying. Marcus couldn't quite put his finger on what it was. 'Some things have to be wrong, though, right?' Marcus replied thoughtfully. 'Like, I love the Breakfast Club Investigators, but I don't think I would do **anything** to keep us together. Sometimes we have to make sure we don't go too far – that's what got us banned in the first place,' he finished sadly.

'Yeah, of course,' Gbenga said quickly. He shook his head. 'You're right. See you later, Marcus – I hope you guys get to the bottom of what's been going on before our match tomorrow.'

Marcus watched Gbenga go, his mind racing with everything he had just said.

As Marcus walked home the heat that had been coursing through him all day slowly faded from his head, leaving the **angry words** behind in his memory. He didn't like what he'd said to Stacey, Lise and Asim, or how he had sounded. But he knew he was right.

Wasn't he?

They didn't need help. After all, Gbenga agreed with him.

Marcus was quiet during dinner. His fork moved slowly from his plate to his mouth on autopilot. But he wasn't really tasting what he was eating.

His mum tried to start a conversation a couple of times, but Marcus just gave monosyllabic answers. He couldn't take his mind off the case.

After dinner, they had their reading hour.

Marcus collapsed down onto his seat with a sigh. He sipped his hot chocolate and opened up his book. He tried to read, tried hard to stop his mind from whirring, but the words just wouldn't go into his brain.

Cursed.

Fifteen minutes later he was still on the same page.

'What's wrong?'

Marcus *jumped* at the sound of his mum's voice, then bit his lip. He wanted to confess all the thoughts that were going around in his head, but he didn't know where to start. 'Nothing,' he said after a long pause, clutching the book closer to his face.

His mum put her book down on the table. 'I'm your mum. I know when it's nothing and I know when something is happening. You've been acting odd all evening. Tell me what's up.'

'It's nothing,' Marcus said once more.

'Come on, you haven't turned a single page since we sat down! You're not reading,' she pressed.

Marcus took a *deep breath.* 'I – I just – I don't need help!' he blurted out.

Her eyes narrowed. 'What do you mean you don't need help? Everyone needs help!'

'I'm sorry, I just . . .' Marcus took in another deep breath and clenched his fists.

'Come over here,' his mum said gently. Marcus got up and walked over to sit by his mum. He leaned against her.

'Talk to me,' she repeated.

'Well . . . it's about my friends. You know,

the Breakfast Club Investigators,' Marcus
began. 'We haven't solved cases for a while
and I thought that if we kept missing out
on these cases, then eventually
everyone would think that

we're not good at solving mysteries and then they wouldn't bring mysteries to us any more. And then our group would fall apart. Because that's why we're together. Mysteries.'

'And?' his mum prompted.

Marcus took a sip of hot chocolate before continuing. 'They want us to ask another club for **HELP,** but if we do, won't everyone just think we're not good?'

His mum sighed heavily. 'Marcus, is that what you really think?'

'Yes.'

She pulled him into a hug. 'Have you tried actually asking your friends what they think? And what they'd do if you stopped having mysteries to work on?' she asked. Marcus shook his head. 'I think you'd get a different answer than you might think. You seem to think that accepting help will make you lesser, but in actual fact being able to ask for help can make you stronger. It doesn't change who you are. It *allows* us to be who we are. When you were a baby who do you think watched you when I went to work?'

'I dunno,' Marcus replied quietly.

'Friends, family, community,' she said, counting off each one on her fingers. 'They helped me. We all need help to achieve the things we want to achieve.'

'But I know people who can do things without any help at all,' Marcus said helplessly.

His mum laughed. 'I promise you this; the people who look like they've had the least amount of help are often the people who've had the **most**.'

Marcus looked up at her with wide eyes. 'Really?' he asked.

'Really,' she said. 'Anyway, it's time to get back to our books. I was actually on a very exciting page.' **They smiled.**

He went back to where he was sitting and picked up his book. He still was having trouble reading, though – he couldn't stop thinking about everything his mum had said.

And as those thoughts circled in his head, he slowly started to think about how they might relate to their case. Maybe, just maybe, they'd be able to *solve it in time.*

Chapter Nineteen

When Marcus arrived at Breakfast Club on Friday, Lise, Stacey and Asim were all sat round with **MISERABLE** looks on their faces.

'We're never going to be able to solve the case in time now,' Stacey moaned as he arrived. The first match of the tournament was that night after school.

Marcus looked around at the three of

them, sitting at their table under the noisy air conditioner, and his heart swelled thinking about the **brilliant adventures** they'd been on. And the ones that were still to come. He couldn't believe he was worried that they would ever not be friends.

'I want to say something,' Marcus said loudly. **'I want to say I'm sorry.** I shouldn't have gotten so mad yesterday. I didn't listen to any of you and—'

'It's OK, Marcus, we understand,' Stacey said, smiling at him.

'No, it's not. It wasn't,' Marcus went on. 'We're the Breakfast Club Investigators. That's who we are. That's what brought us together.' Marcus's mouth felt dry, but he knew that he had to continue. 'I felt like if we admitted that we needed help, then we would be bad at being Investigators. And if we weren't the Breakfast Club Investigators, then maybe we would all **fall apart**.'

Stacey frowned. 'You really thought that?'

Marcus nodded.

'The Breakfast Club Investigators is what brought us together, but that's not what kept us together after our first case. It's not what keeps us together now even though Mrs Miller has banned us from the school,' Stacey said.

'We don't hang out with you because we like investigating stuff,' said Asim, grinning.

'We do it because we're **friends**!' Lise punched him gently on the shoulder.

'That bond can't be broken. No matter what happens to the Breakfast Club Investigators,' Stacey proclaimed.

Marcus looked at the friends around him. They were all smiling at him, so he began to smile too.

'Yeah, I think I see that now,' Marcus said.

'Good, so **apology accepted** from my end. What about the rest of you?' Stacey turned to Asim and Lise.

'Apology accepted,' Lise said almost immediately.

Asim's eyes **narrowed.** 'Apology accepted – but you owe me something. I haven't decided what, yet, but you definitely owe me something.'

There was a mischievous smile on his face.

'All right.' Marcus rolled his eyes, and then he began to laugh. Stacey, Lise and Asim joined in, and for a moment, laughter was all that could be heard on their table.

When their laughter finally died down, Stacey leaned in. The glint was back in her eye once again. 'So, I guess it's time to finally talk to the Journalism Club?' she asked.

Marcus smiled ruefully. 'I think you're right,' he said. *It's definitely time.*

The group walked over to the other side of the canteen, where Maxine was sitting, scribbling furiously in a notepad and eating a stack of buttered toast. She looked up as they approached, regarding them suspiciously.

'What are you doing here?' Maxine said.

'We're mostly here to apologize,' Marcus

replied. 'We've been pretty rude to you over the last couple of days. I wanted to say I'm sorry.'

'We're also here to ask for your help,' Stacey said, **poking** her head over Marcus's shoulder.

Maxine grinned up at them. 'Well, apology accepted! Come on, take a seat.' Maxine pointed at free chairs around the table. 'Why were you so sure we were behind the Ghoul anyway?'

'Well, we found a Journalism Club pin in the gym, near a bottle filled with ectoplasm,' Stacey said.

'Ectoplasm?' Maxine asked, raising an eyebrow.

'Spooky, thick liquid left behind by supernatural beings,' Lise explained.

'Although I actually think it could have been **jelly**,' Marcus interjected.

Maxine frowned at them all. 'You really think we'd drop a pin of ours near a piece of evidence, and leave it in exactly the right place for you to find?'

Marcus stared at her. Now that he thought about it, it seemed obvious that the Journalism Club wouldn't do that – had he been too swept up in their rivalry to see what was right in front of him?

'**Someone's setting us up**,' Maxine went on. 'Are we on such bad terms that you'd think we'd deliberately set out to mess up your investigations?' There was a trace of sadness in her voice. 'Maybe we are. I was a little mean the last time we talked.' She said that last part under her breath, seemingly to herself even though everyone else could hear what she was saying.

'More than a little,' Asim said. 'But we were rude too. I guess we should have just understood that we were both working towards the same goal, and we could have helped each other all along instead of being in competition.'

'We could have been a *dream team!*' Stacey smiled.

'Maybe we still can be,' Lise nodded.

Maxine grinned at them all. 'An excellent point!' she said loudly. Marcus suppressed a grin of his own – he had a feeling Maxine was enjoying this. 'OK, as a symbol of goodwill I'll answer any questions you may have about, well, **ANYTHING!**'

Marcus took a deep breath. Even though

he knew what he needed to ask, the words didn't come easily. 'Well . . .' he started, 'the thing you talked about before. Why you've been able to solve cases and we haven't. You said you had an idea of why that might be?'

Maxine **leaned backwards,** regarding him with interest. She took a bite of toast. 'It's because it's just you,' she said after a few moments. 'Just the four of you. Now, don't get me wrong – I'm not saying you need to have a **MILLION** members, it's just that if you're only going to have four members, you're going to miss things. There's always going to be something that you don't understand.'

Marcus still didn't really understand.

Maxine continued, 'It's like how Sypha in the Archive Club helped me research the old

Journalism Club magazine issues, so I could find the article about the old basketball team. And it's like how Martin in the Cooking Club is helping me with the **BRUISED BANANAS** case.'

A light had suddenly flicked on in Marcus's brain. Maxine's words sounded a lot like his mum's last night.

He stared at the ground. 'I didn't even know those clubs existed,' Marcus admitted.

'There's a whole world of people in this school who each have so much information. If you want to be good at *investigating,* you can't afford not to make those friends – I always need to ask for help.' Maxine finished with a smile on her face.

Marcus's face felt **HOT.** He looked around at Stacey, Lise and Asim, worried that they would be angry with him – after all, Marcus had been the one who was determined that the Breakfast Club Investigators could solve the case without any help.

'That makes total sense,' Stacey said to Maxine, nodding. 'So, now can you tell us what you found out about the old basketball team?'

'Well, I found the captain of the Rutherford Rhinos!' Maxine said excitedly. 'It turns out he **didn't curse the team.** It was just a rumour at the time, and the school newspaper took the rumour and ran with it because they thought it would make a great story.' Maxine looked disapproving.

Marcus felt **dazed.** 'So, are you saying that the curse *doesn't* exist?'

'But that's impossible!' Stacey exclaimed.

'We are definitely cursed!'

Maxine was silent for a moment. 'Well . . . were you cursed or did you just *think* you were cursed?'

'What?' Asim gaped at her.

'Let's try something,' Maxine said. She looked at Marcus, Stacey, Lise and Asim one by one. 'Clear your mind. Now – don't think about **elephants**.' She paused. 'What animal are you all thinking about?'

'Elephants,' the group said all at once.

Maxine grinned. 'Your mind is a **powerful** thing – if you think you're cursed and that idea gets into your head, it can affect you in all sorts of ways, even though nothing's actually happening.'

'Wait, so I can actually still paint?' Asim said hopefully.

'Of course you can!' Maxine beamed at him.

Stacey **slapped** her hand to her forehead. 'I've just remembered! I spilt some tea on my book – *that's* why I didn't have it. It was drying out at home. I just forgot!' Stacey exclaimed. Then she frowned. 'But what about the ectoplasm we found outside our hideout?'

Lise shook her head. 'There has to be another explanation for it . . .'

Marcus felt stunned. They'd been working so hard over the last couple of weeks trying to solve this mystery, and it felt like the entire time they had been running around in circles while Maxine did the real investigating. And now they'd run out of time.

Maxine put a hand on his shoulder. **'Mysteries are hard, guys.** I was only able to help and come up with the clue about the Rutherford Rhinos because you did a bunch of investigating beforehand,' she said. There was sympathy on her face, but that just made Marcus feel even worse.

'But we'll still never be able to solve the case in time!' he exploded. 'The basketball tournament starts tonight, and we still don't know who's been **haunting** the team!

We still don't know who the Ghoul is.'

'Well . . .' Maxine said slowly. 'Why don't we think about this together? Who'd have something to gain from both the curse and the Ghoul?'

The five of them all looked at each other, thinking hard.

'Someone who wanted the basketball team to be bad,' Asim piped up.

'And not just bad, but bad in a way that attracts attention,' Lise said slowly.

'They'd want to keep people away from the gym at night. That's when the Ghoul struck the first time, right?' Stacey said. 'So, they'd need access to the school gym.'

'The Ghoul also struck during basketball team games,' Maxine added.

'And don't forget about the journalism pin next to the ectoplasm. We trust you, Maxine, but not all the members of the Journalism Club,' Stacey said with a **wink.**

And with that, something suddenly clunked into place in Marcus's head. 'I have an idea,' he said slowly. 'But it doesn't

explain everything. Listen –' And the group *leaned in*, listening intently to Marcus as he told them his theory.

Chapter Twenty

Marcus, Stacey, Asim, Lise and Maxine stood just inside the school entrance. Classes were finished and students were milling around or heading home to have dinner before returning for the game. Tonight, at 7 p.m., the basketball tournament would begin. They had to stop the Ghoul here. It was now or never.

'Remember to meet back here every ten

minutes,' Stacey said to the group as the crowd around them thinned. 'If one of us isn't here then we'll know that something bad has happened.'

Lise nodded. Asim gulped. The words *something bad* echoed through Marcus's head. His mouth started to feel dry, the nerves **bubbling** up again.

Maxine winked at the Breakfast Club Investigators. 'Come on, guys,' she said. 'This is it – we'll definitely catch the Ghoul now we're working together.'

Marcus smiled **nervously** at her. It did make him feel a little more confident, knowing they had one more person on their side.

At Stacey's signal, the five of them **split up,** each going their own way through the maze of now-empty school corridors.

Stacey had said that splitting up would be the best way to tempt the Ghoul out – after all, what better **bait** is there than one person on their own?

As Marcus walked down the empty corridors, alone, all he could hear was the sound of his breath. Each turn felt like an opportunity for something bad to happen. He could swear that the steady rhythm of his heart was getting **faster** with every step he took. A quickly **growing gloom** spread as the sun set, making it even harder to see things.

After ten minutes of nervously stalking the hallways, it was time to meet up with the rest of the Investigators. Feeling a mixture of disappointment and relief, Marcus made his way back to the school entrance.

Stacey and Asim were already there, peering around anxiously.

'Did you find anything?' Stacey whispered as soon as she saw him.

Marcus shook his head.

'Neither of us saw anything either,' said Asim. He looked as relieved as Marcus felt.

'How *unlucky* can we be?' Stacey stamped her foot in frustration.

The three of them stood in tense silence as they waited for Lise and Maxine to arrive, growing more nervous as each minute passed.

'Aren't they supposed to be back by now?' Marcus asked eventually.

'Something bad must have happened to them,' Asim breathed, a look of terror on his face. **'The Ghoul must have got them!'**

'We have to find them!' Stacey tore off down the hallway, with Marcus and Asim hot on her heels.

They rushed down the stairs and through the hallways. At first, they tried to not make too much noise and alert any remaining teachers, but as each new turn showed another empty corridor and their **PANIC** grew, they began moving more quickly. Their loud footsteps crashed up and around them as they called out for Lise and Maxine.

Just when Marcus began to think that they may have to change their tactics, they heard a noise up ahead.

'Stop, don't get any closer!' Lise's voice rang out down one of the corridors not far from where they were. Marcus turned to Asim and Stacey, his eyes wide. Wordlessly, he pointed at the corridor to their right, and they ran towards the sound.

They found Lise crouched in a corner of the hallway with her hands over her eyes. In front of her was a tall shadowy figure.

The Ghoul.

'Lise!' Stacey cried as soon as she saw her.

Asim rushed to put a protective arm around her shoulders, while Stacey forced herself between Lise and the Ghoul.

Marcus pushed down his rising fear and went to stand beside Stacey.

The Ghoul took a *threatening* step towards them. But then Stacey said something that stopped it dead.

'We know who you are.'

The Ghoul **howled.**

Marcus took a nervous step forward.

'We know who you really are,' he said.

It was as if time stopped.

For a moment, no one moved.

It was then that the Ghoul did the thing they least expected. It turned around and **ran.**

Chapter Twenty-One

Marcus, Lise, Asim and Stacey tore after it. They followed the Ghoul through the hallways, chasing it up and down stairs.

But the Ghoul seemed to have incredibly long legs; it was as if it was *gliding* away from them.

Marcus sucked in deep breaths while he tried his hardest to keep his legs pumping. Behind him, he could tell that Stacey, Lise and Asim were exhausted by their heavy breathing, but they were keeping up, just about. **Marcus knew they didn't have much time left.**

'It's time to activate phase two of the plan,' Marcus yelled over the crashing sound of footsteps.

'Roger!' Stacey, Lise and Asim shouted back, and they split off, each running down a different hallway. Suddenly Marcus was all alone, chasing the Ghoul by himself.

A few moments later, the Ghoul started to turn down a corridor to its left, but suddenly *whipped* around and changed direction.

As Marcus ran past he glanced down the corridor to his left and saw Asim. He had stopped the Ghoul escaping that way.

The Ghoul sprinted down the corridor on

its right, but suddenly two figures appeared at the end of it, blocking its way. It was Stacey and Lise.

The Ghoul stopped, panting hard. It turned slowly in a circle, looking utterly lost. **It was trapped.**

Suddenly it bent over with its hands on its knees. It pressed its back against the wall and then slid down to the floor.

Marcus, Stacey, Lise and Asim bore down on it from different directions.

'It's not a real Ghoul, is it?' Stacey breathed when they were in front of it. Now that the lights were on and Marcus was up close to the Ghoul, he could see that it was a suit. A costume of stitched-together grey cloth. Around the Ghoul's head was a mask.

Marcus felt kind of bad for Stacey – just

like with the chupacabra, it looked like the Ghoul wasn't a **supernatural** creature after all.

'I don't think so,' Lise said apologetically.

'This is a good thing, Stacey,' Asim said, clapping her on the shoulder. 'It means we're not going to get eaten.'

'I guess.' Stacey looked forlorn. Then she steeled herself. 'I think it's time to find out if our theory is right.' She waved Marcus forward. **'I'll let you do the honours.'**

Marcus turned to the Ghoul. He took a small step towards it, then reached out a trembling hand. It was silly – even though Marcus knew that it wasn't a real Ghoul, he still felt a little bit *hesitant.* But he pushed through it. He was a Breakfast Club Investigator, after all.

He reached down and **ripped off** the Ghoul's mask.

They all gasped.

Gbenga blinked hard as his eyes adjusted to the light. He didn't say anything. There was a pitiful look on his face, like he had always expected it to end this way.

Gbenga looked at Marcus and hung his head. Even though he had suspected Gbenga, Marcus had never seen him look so **small.**

'Why did you do it, Gbenga?' Marcus whispered.

Gbenga didn't raise his eyes from the floor. He started speaking in a quiet voice. 'It wasn't on purpose, I promise. **This all just got away from me**.' He took a deep breath.

Stacey sat down on the floor next to him. 'Why don't you tell us how it started,' she said kindly.

Gbenga was quiet for a moment, like he was trying to find the words. 'I – well, I used to stay late in the gym. Training and, you know, trying my best to get better. But I didn't want everyone to know that. I didn't want anyone to know how hard I had to work.'

Marcus frowned. An uncomfortable feeling of recognition was stirring in his stomach. This was exactly how he had felt about the Breakfast Club Investigators.

'Why not?' Asim asked.

'You don't know what it's like to be a captain of a team,' Gbenga said, wringing his hands desperately. 'We can't just be a normal member of the team, we have to be *better*. We have to be *the best*. I felt like if people knew how hard I had to work to do that, then maybe **they wouldn't believe in me.**' Gbenga's eyes were sparkling. It looked like he was trying hard not to cry.

Lise slapped her forehead. 'So, you were training in **secret**!' she exclaimed. 'That's why we found those uniforms with all the liquid on them. And we thought it was ectoplasm.'

'Except it wasn't ectoplasm,' Marcus

took over. 'It would have been sweat at first, before you poured that jelly onto it.' It was all coming together in his head. 'You were trying to make it look like something it wasn't.' He crouched down next to Gbenga.

'But how did things turn from you training secretly to becoming a Ghoul? That's a **pretty big jump**,' Asim said, scratching his head.

Gbenga bit his lip. 'It was an accident. I was wearing dark clothes, trying to sneak out after a late-night practice. Georgina saw me and got **scared.** The whole team were talking about it the next day. That's when the plan sort of came together – if I could just dress up every once in a while and get everyone spooked, I'd have the gym all to myself after school.'

'But things got *out of control*,' said Marcus.

Gbenga sighed. 'Before I knew it, the whole team thought there was a **curse,** and that there was a **Ghoul.** There had been rumours of a curse on the team in the past, so it all came together. But it went wrong. The team were **SPOOKED,** and that meant that we weren't able to play as well.'

'But why did you ask us for help investigating your own crimes?' Marcus said with raised eyebrows.

'The team begged me to do it. The Ghoul and curse got into their heads. We all heard how you solved that other case, and I thought it would make everyone less suspicious of me. All I had to do was **scare you off,** but you didn't get scared, you kept on investigating,' Gbenga said miserably.

'Being stubborn is kind of our thing,' Lise said with a grin.

'Gbenga,' Marcus began softly, **'you just needed to ask for help.** You didn't need to be ashamed that you were putting in extra practice . We all have to try hard to get good at the things we care about.'

'But we're a good team,' Gbenga protested. 'That's what everyone knows us as, if we ask for help, then . . .' Gbenga trailed off, clearly lost for words.

'You'll still be a good team,' Marcus said confidently. 'No one will judge you for asking for help. We all need help sometimes. I had to figure that out myself.'

Gbenga's head dropped. He looked so pitiful, huddled on the floor in his grey costume. Marcus felt sorry for him.

'But what about during the basketball games?' Stacey piped up suddenly. 'The Ghoul appeared when you were playing, how did that happen?'

Gbenga frowned. 'What are you talking about?' he said. 'I thought the Ghoul appearing at matches was something the team was just imagining – that they were making the Ghoul into something it wasn't, and seeing things . . .'

'But that doesn't make any sense – we *saw* the Ghoul during the basketball game on Monday,' said Marcus. He was starting to feel very confused.

'You did?' Gbenga looked shocked.

'How could that have been Gbenga?' Asim said, rubbing his chin. 'He was playing in the game at the time.'

Gbenga was looking up at them all with wide eyes.

Marcus sat back on his heels, thinking hard.

'What if,' he said slowly, 'what if there was **someone else** involved? Someone who had something else to gain from the presence of the Ghoul.'

Gbenga shook his head in disbelief.

Just then, there was a **yell** from somewhere up ahead.

Chapter Twenty-Two

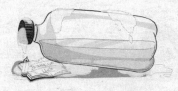

Marcus, Stacey, Lise, Asim and Gbenga all exchanged wide-eyed glances. Without a word, Marcus, Stacey and Gbenga got to their feet, and the five of them raced down the corridor towards the noise.

Just around the corner, an unexpected sight greeted their eyes.

It was Maxine. She was struggling as she *pinned* something – or someone – to the ground.

'*Maxine!*' Marcus exclaimed. 'What's going on?' He looked at Stacey, who appeared to be just as confused as he was. The five of

them slowly approached Maxine, and as they did Marcus could finally make out what she was pinning to the ground.

He gasped.

'This doesn't make sense,' Gbenga said.

'Don't just stand there, I could do with some help!' Maxine shouted. Stacey and Marcus hurried over. Underneath Maxine was a **second Ghoul.**

Together, Marcus and Stacey grabbed the Ghoul by the arms and dragged it over to the wall, where it sat, looking extremely miserable. It pulled its knees up to its chest.

Marcus looked between Gbenga and the second Ghoul, thinking hard.

Maxine was staring at Gbenga, who was still wearing his Ghoul costume. 'Oh, Gbenga,' she said sadly.

Gbenga looked down at the floor.

'It does kind of make sense,' Marcus said slowly. 'The **evidence**, the motivations. There had to be multiple people behind this.'

'I guess it's smart having two of them. Not smart enough to beat us, though.' Stacey grinned.

'Not when the Journalism Club and the Breakfast Club Investigators are on the job!' Maxine exclaimed.

'But **who's behind the second mask**?' Asim piped up.

Wordlessly, Marcus walked towards the second Ghoul and pulled off the mask.

There was a loud intake of breath.

It was Noah. He scowled up at the group around him, but didn't say anything.

'**Noah!**' Maxine yelped. 'I should have known!' She ground her teeth in frustration. 'But why? Why would you do this?'

Noah was quiet for a moment. Then he said in a surly voice, 'I wanted to make a good story.'

It was the first time Marcus had actually heard him speak.

Maxine **threw up her hands in** disbelief. 'All this for a good story!'

Lise was frowning at him. 'So you heard rumours of the Ghoul haunting Basketball Club, and you wanted to turn it into a real thing? You wanted the legend of the Ghoul to come to life?'

Noah *glared* at her, and then gave a terse nod.

'But what about the Journalism Club badge that we found next to the ectoplasm?' Marcus interjected.

'I wanted you to suspect the Journalism Club, so you wouldn't work with us and could never solve the case,' Noah mumbled.

'Woah,' breathed Gbenga. 'This has gotten **SO** out of hand.'

Marcus nodded in agreement, still staring wide-eyed at Noah in the Ghoul costume. He wanted to ask him more questions, but it was clear that he didn't want to talk any more. Maxine was still glaring at him.

Suddenly, Stacey called out, 'Hey, did we just solve a mystery?' Her eyes were **shining**.

'I think we did,' said Asim. He **punched** the air.

'Good work, team!' Lise yelled.

Marcus couldn't keep the smile off his face. 'I'm happy we solved the mystery, but I think there's still one more thing to do.'

'And what's that?' Stacey asked.

Chapter
Twenty-Three

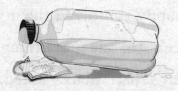

Three days later

Mrs Miller was leaning back in her chair, looking very comfortable. Marcus, Stacey, Asim and Lise were lined up in a row in front of her desk as usual, but the atmosphere was different now. More relaxed.

The school basketball team had played their first match of the tournament last Friday, right after the Breakfast Club Investigators had caught the '**Ghouls**'. They had ended up losing, although the team had played a lot more confidently now that they knew the curse wasn't real.

After the group had solved the case, they had told Mr Anderson what they knew. Gbenga and Noah had each received a couple of weeks' worth of detention, and Mr Anderson put in a good word for the Breakfast Club Investigators with Mrs Miller.

'So, are we reinstated as a club?' Stacey said.

Mrs Miller smiled at her. 'Well, you all did an **excellent job** in solving what was going on with the basketball team.' Then her smile faded and she shook her head. 'Gbenga and Noah, I never would have believed it.' She sighed. 'You've shown me that it might actually be useful to have some investigators at our school. But I will be keeping an eye on you from now on. You can't go around ruining school events. You're still on *thin ice*.'

The four of them nodded in unison.

'We are sorry about that, Mrs Miller,' said Marcus. 'We were just desperate to solve this case.'

'What else were we supposed to do?' Asim said in a small voice.

Mrs Miller sighed again. 'Me, Mr Anderson, the entire school — we're always here to help,' she said. 'Maybe just ask us for help next time, instead of crashing into school events.'

It wasn't the first time over the last couple of days that Marcus had heard those words, but he was surprised to hear them from Mrs Miller.

'Yes, Mrs Miller,' the investigators said at once.

'We'll be on our best behaviour,' Stacey added, trying to look convincingly abashed.

Marcus could tell Mrs Miller didn't buy it for a second. 'You'd better be,' she said, with a steely look in her eye.

As soon as Mrs Miller had dismissed them from her office, the group made their way up to the English classroom. Maxine waved at them as they walked in.

'We just wanted to say thank you for helping us with the Ghoul case,' Marcus said.

'No need to thank me.' Maxine shook

her head. 'I still can't believe Noah was involved, and just so we could get more readers! Maybe we need to get out of the *mystery investigation game* and get back to good old-fashioned journalism.' But there was a dark twinkle in her eyes. 'But first, we have so much material for next month's article: an interview with the captain of the **RUTHERFORD**

RHINOS, and the behind-the-scenes story of how **Rutherford's Ghouls** were finally unmasked! We're going to be getting through copies like hot cakes!' She rubbed her hands together with a grin.

Stacey, Lise and Asim all laughed, but Marcus stayed quiet – something was on his mind.

'You know, I was talking to Gbenga the entire time that we were working on the case,' Marcus said quietly. 'I felt like I could talk to him about the BCI splitting up.'

Lise looked at him sadly. 'Did he say anything that made you think it was him?' she asked eventually.

'**I can't really tell** . . .' Marcus said.

'I can't stop thinking about Noah,' Maxine said, with understanding in her eyes. 'If I'd just listened to him and never reached out to you guys, then . . .'

'We would have never solved the case,' Asim finished grimly.

'I just wish he felt he could have asked for help, especially when he was finding things so hard,' Marcus said, his mind still on Gbenga.

'Gbenga and Noah, even though they were both the Ghoul, they never figured that out or asked each other for help,' Stacey said, rubbing her chin. 'I don't think we would have ever caught them if they were properly working together.

'And the only reason we ended up catching them was because **we did work together**.' Maxine smiled.

'We need to work together more often,' Marcus said excitedly.

'And I have the perfect place to start. I've got a lead on the bruised banana case, and I could really use your help.'

They all grinned at each other.

'Let's get to work!' exclaimed Marcus.

About the Authors

Marcus Rashford MBE

Marcus Rashford MBE is Manchester United's iconic number 10 and an England International footballer.

During the lockdown imposed due to the COVID-19 pandemic, Marcus teamed up with the food distribution charity FareShare to cover the free school meal deficit for vulnerable children across the UK, raising in excess of £20 million. Marcus successfully lobbied the British Government to u-turn policy around the free food voucher programme – a campaign that has been deemed the quickest turnaround of government policy in the history of British politics – so that 1.3 million vulnerable children continued to have access to food supplies whilst schools were closed during the pandemic.

In response to Marcus's End Child Food Poverty campaign, the British Government committed £400 million to support vulnerable children across the UK, supporting 1.7 million children for the next 12 months.

In October 2020, he was appointed MBE in the Queen's Birthday Honours. Marcus has committed himself to combating child poverty in the UK and his other books, including *You Are a Champion,* are inspiring guides for children about reaching their full potential.

Alex Falase-Koya

Alex Falase-Koya is a London native. He has been both reading and writing since he was a teenager; anything at the cross-section of social commentary and genre fiction floats his boat. He was a winner of Spread the Word's 2019 London Writers Awards for YA/children's. He now lives in Walthamstow with his girlfriend and two cats. He is the co-writer of Marcus Rashford's children's fiction series *The Breakfast Club Adventures*.

About the Illustrator

Marta Kissi

Marta Kissi studied BA Illustration & Animation at Kingston University and MA Visual Communication at the Royal College of Art. Her favourite part of being an illustrator is bringing stories to life by designing charming characters and the wonderful worlds they live in. She shares a studio with her husband James.

THE MARCUS RASHFORD BOOK CLUB

The Marcus Rashford Book Club is a collaboration between Marcus Rashford MBE and Macmillan Children's Books, helping children aged 8–12 to develop literacy as a life skill and a love of reading. Two books will be chosen each year by Marcus and the Macmillan team, one in summer and another in the autumn, with the mission to increase children's access to books outside of school. The book club will feature an exciting selection of titles, which aim to make every child feel supported, represented and empowered.

The book club launched in June 2021, with the fully illustrated, laugh-out-loud, time-travel adventure, *A Dinosaur Ate My Sister* by Pooja Puri, illustrated by Allen Fatimaharan, followed by *Silas and the Marvellous Misfits* by Tom Percival, an action-packed, fully-illustrated adventure that shows kids the joy of being themselves. Copies of these books will be available in shops, and to ensure all children have access to them, free copies will also be distributed to support under-privileged and vulnerable children across the UK.

magic
breakfast
fuel for learning

You know what happens when a car runs out of fuel or battery power don't you, it just stops! Well, it's pretty much the same for people. When we don't have enough food or drink inside us, we don't have the energy we need to be able to do all the things we want and need to do in a day, like playing with friends, learning maths, or reading a favourite book. It is also really important that the food we eat is healthy, not too full of sugar, and gives us energy that will last the whole day.

Eating breakfast is particularly important as it will probably have been a long time since our last meal, so there won't be a lot of energy left in our bodies to help us learn. Magic Breakfast is a charity that works with lots of schools in England and Scotland to help them make sure all their pupils eat a healthy breakfast, so they are full of energy for the morning ahead.

Magic Breakfast is very pleased to have joined Marcus Rashford and Macmillan Children's Books to ensure thousands of schoolchildren from its partner schools receive books from Marcus Rashford's Book Club. Together we can provide breakfast to fuel learning and books to transport you to new worlds, especially for those who may have neither at home.

Magic Breakfast would also like to thank Marsh for all their support and their generous contribution to support our continued involvement in this initiative.

To learn more about Magic Breakfast you can visit their website: **www.magicbreakfast.com** and remember, always have breakfast at home or at school if you can.

Being able to read, write, speak and listen well can change someone's life: these skills don't just help throughout school and work, they also support overall well-being. Books and reading are a brilliant way to boost these important literacy skills, but unfortunately the National Literacy Trust research shows that an estimated 410,000 children don't own a single book of their own. The charity is a proud partner of Marcus Rashford's Book Club to help provide children and young people with access to books and their life-changing benefits.

It's the National Literacy Trust's mission to improve the literacy levels of those who need support most. It runs Literacy Hubs and campaigns with schools and families in communities where low literacy seriously impact people's life chances. The charity has a huge range of literacy-building resources and activities online for children and young people of all ages, including complementary resources for this brilliant new Book Club.

www.literacytrust.org.uk

Hello!

Did you enjoy *The Breakfast Club Adventures*?

At KPMG we love books and the exciting new worlds they can open up to us all. That's why we're happy to support the Marcus Rashford Book Club, so that more children have access to books at school and at home.

We hope you really enjoyed your new book.

Happy reading!
From everyone at KPMG UK.